Above the Law

Editor: Talia Leduc

ISBN-13: 9781990590207

Give feedback on the book at:
lorhainneeckhart@hotmail.com

Twitter: @LEckhart
Facebook: AuthorLorhainneEckhart

Printed in the U.S.A

ABOVE THE LAW

Billy Jo McCabe Mystery

LORHAINNE ECKHART

The Billy Jo McCabe Mystery

Nothing As It Seems
Hiding in Plain Sight
The Cold Case
The Trap
Above the Law
The Stranger at the Door
The Children
The Last Stand

A Billy Jo McCabe Mystery Box Set: Books 1 - 3
A Billy Jo McCabe Mystery Box Set: Books 4 - 6

The social worker and the cop, an unlikely couple drawn together on a small, secluded Pacific Northwest island where nothing is as it seems. Protecting the innocent comes at a cost, and what seems to be a sleepy, quiet town is anything but.

The Social Worker

Billy Jo McCabe wants only to help children overcome their troubled lives, as she herself struggles to forget the childhood nightmare she survived. She took sociology and prelaw at the insistence of her adoptive father, Chase McCabe, and learned how to use power tools from her adoptive mother, Rose. She loves reading in the backs of bookstores before tucking the book back on the shelf and slipping out without paying. She has a fondness for peanut butter and dill pickle sandwiches, has a three-legged cat named Harley, hates running (because that was all she did as a kid), and secretly binges on brownies and red wine on the sofa in front of her TV every Friday night.

She's never been married and has dated only twice. She visits Chase and Rose when summoned and shows up dutifully for every holiday with her family, but she has no siblings to speak of, and she feels a growing resentment for the mother who abandoned her in foster care. Despite proudly maintaining the same prickly attitude that nearly landed her behind bars as a kid, she has yet to speak up to Chase, who interferes in her life too frequently, ready to fix every problem, whether she wants him to or not.

One thing no one knows about Billy Jo is that she moved to Roche Harbor because it's the only clue she has about the last known whereabouts of the woman who abandoned her.

The Cop

Mark Friessen, son of Jed and Diana Friessen, has landed accidently in the role of small-town detective, a position in which he's going nowhere. Nearly married once, and broken-hearted three times, he's sworn he'll stay single forever, and he keeps his tattoo of a former girlfriend as a reminder that only fools fall in love. He's tall, attractive, and stubborn, and he refuses to live in the shadow of his two older brothers, Chris and Danny.

As Roche Harbor's youngest detective, he sleeps with a gun under his pillow. He has a stray dog that won't leave, and he swears that the only two food groups that exist are meat and potatoes. His favorite drink is black coffee in the morning, sugared coffee in the afternoon, and a shot of whiskey in his coffee at night to keep him warm.

****Each book in this series is a complete book, with no cliff-hangers, and can be read as a standalone. However, these books may contain references to situations from earlier books in the series. As with any long book series that focuses on specific characters, their changing relationships, and how their lives continue to unfold, you may find it more enjoyable to read the series in order of publishing, as there will be developments and changes in the relationship dynamics of the core characters.*

"You know there hasn't been a story in this series that hasn't had a powerful message, and this one is no exception...a fascinating story that will catch your attention at the beginning and hold on to it until the very end."

Catlou, Reviewer

"A riveting book...very timely and eye opening."

Irish Eyes 430, Reviewer

His crime was unforgivable, but the law protects him.

If an alleged crime is reported to you, but no victim can be found, has a crime been committed? This is exactly the question Billy Jo McCabe asks Detective Mark Friessen when an anonymous woman approaches her and tells her about an unspeakable crime taking place right under the watch of the chief of police, in his own family.

When Billy Jo reaches out to Mark with the story, he just can't look away. They soon learn family is family, and the victim has been hiding her secret for years. But she's not just any victim: She's Cheyenne Potter, the niece of the chief of police, Tolly Shephard.

Mark has always suspected Tolly is a man of many secrets. Because he just can't sit by, he partners up with Billy Jo to dig into the chief, his family, and the secret they're hiding. He's convinced the chief helped bury a crime, but every answer they find only exposes another question. The players in this game are people who use the law to their advantage, and even though neither Mark nor Billy Jo is afraid of a fight, they soon learn that stepping on the wrong toes may lead them into a fight they can't win. Sometimes the law doesn't protect the innocent—and it has the best nondisclosures money can buy.

Chapter 1

"You ready to go?" Mark called out the minute he stepped into her place.

No "Hi." No "How are you?" It was always "Hurry up, already."

Billy Jo stared at the makeup she'd been about to put on, then tossed it back in her makeup bag, untouched. What had she been thinking, forking over her hard-earned cash on a whim for something she never wore?

"Seriously, Billy Jo, what are you doing?" she said to her reflection in the mirror as she flicked her hands through her plain and boring shoulder-length brown hair, noting the freckles that dotted her nose.

She'd never be the supermodel type. So, again, why was she doing this?

"Hey, didn't you hear me? What are you doing in here?" Mark said as he strolled in.

She stared up at the tall, rugged, arrogant cowboy. His new jean jacket didn't quite match his faded blue jeans, and his wavy red hair was short and appeared freshly cut. The way he talked to her, it was always as if he didn't have a clue what she was thinking. He rested his hand on the doorframe and took in her small bathroom.

"I'm doing what a girl does: getting ready," she said. "You said dinner at that new Mexican place. You made a reservation?"

He stepped back from the doorway, dragging his gaze down, taking in her new sleeveless black blouse and dressy capris, a gift from her mom. He had her feeling both uncomfortable and awkward.

"What?" She knew it came out quite sharply.

There was the pull of his lips, the smile that wasn't really a smile but rather a sign of his amusement at her expense. Maybe that was why she could feel the frown knitting her brow.

"Didn't say anything," he said. "And no, didn't get around to making a reservation. We don't need it."

She wondered at times what it was about him that had her wanting to pull her hair out. "It's new and it's busy. We need a reservation or it's going to be fish tacos at the stand again—and I'd rather not, if it's all the same to you."

He only angled his head, those blue eyes flickering, too good to look at. She knew he would rather argue than just go along with what he was supposed to do. But that seemed to be who they were and how this thing, whatever this was between them, worked.

"You worry too much," he said.

At the jab, she felt her hands fisting at her sides. "And you seem to think we can just walk right in there and…what, we'll be given a table?"

He flicked his jacket back as if trying to make a

point, resting his hand right beside his badge, tucked into the waistband of his jeans. He said nothing.

"You seriously think you can just show your badge and they'll bump us right to the front of the line?" she said.

He made a rude noise, one she'd heard from him too many times when she just didn't go along with his way of thinking. "You make it sound like a bad thing. Everyone knows who I am…"

She could tell exactly what he'd been thinking by the way he trailed off. "And you don't think there's anything wrong with that? Walking right in, past all the people who actually thought ahead to make reservations, past anyone else waiting their turn on the list? You seriously think that just because you're a cop here, you get priority?" She flicked off the light in the bathroom and stepped out.

He suddenly seemed at a loss for words. "Now, wait a second. That wasn't what I meant."

She angled her head. He stepped back, and she walked around him to the island, where her cell phone was plugged in and charging. She took a second to check that it was in the green, at one hundred percent. As she looked over, she thought he dropped an F-bomb under his breath before pulling his cell phone from his pocket and dialing.

"Yeah, this is Detective Mark Friessen. This is probably short notice, but do you have a table available for dinner for two? I was planning on coming now and just showing up, but it was pointed out to me that you're likely busy, and…"

She could hear someone talking on the other end.

"Uh-huh," was all Mark said. As he flicked his gaze

over to her, his blue eyes seemed to simmer with something. "Sounds great. We're on our way," he said, then hung up and tucked his phone in his pocket.

She stared at what seemed to be smugness in his expression.

"Apparently there's always a table available for me," he said. Then he shrugged. "I called like you said. You should be happy now." He gestured as if she'd made a big deal out of nothing.

"Yet you just couldn't help yourself from using your detective title before asking for a table," she said. "Mark, it's the same as if you'd walked in there and flashed your badge. Ever heard of abuse of authority? There shouldn't always be a table for you. That is very much someone giving you something for a favor." She tucked her phone in her bag.

He narrowed his gaze. "I am the last person to use my position to get something. Seriously, I don't work that way. I can't be bought and don't give out special favors. You're making it sound as if I'm taking a kickback or something. I pay my own way. I don't take gifts or bribes."

She pulled her arms over her chest, taking in how defensive he suddenly sounded. "I hate to tell you this, but a table in a crowded restaurant is a kickback, whatever you want to call it, if you got it using your position in the community."

"Do you want me to cancel? Is that what this is?"

She realized in that second that he didn't get it. He stared at her with what she thought was the usual frustration that happened in their discussions, where she had one idea and he seemed to pull counterarguments from his ass.

"No, I'm hungry," she said. "Let's go."

He stood there for a second as if he didn't believe her. "There's a test in here, right?"

She didn't smile. She didn't say anything. She simply took in her three-legged cat, Harley, as he hopped up onto the sofa. Mark looked down at her with the same kind of apprehension with which he might have looked at a ticking timebomb.

"Don't look so worried," she finally said. "Let's go. But hear me on this: If we get there and there's a crowd waiting, and, sure enough, they've bumped you to the front of the line because of your phone call, you say no to the table and ask them to put us in the queue, where we should have been to begin with."

He lifted his hands as if surrendering. "Fine. Point made," he said, then gestured to the door.

Billy Jo had to remind herself that it wasn't healthy to enjoy this butting of heads that seemed to come naturally between her and Mark.

Chapter 2

The sun was going down. Mark took in his watch, noting that it was approaching eight thirty. He had to remind himself to fight the instinct to go back over to the hostess just inside the door, who still had a spooked expression.

Billy Jo had been right. Maybe that was why he was so uncomfortable as he sat outside on the bench, because he'd done what Billy Jo had expected and asked the hostess whether she'd bumped him to the front of the line, ahead of the dozen or so people already waiting, just because he was Detective Friessen.

What had her answer been? She had stared in horror, because apparently he wasn't supposed to have asked that. Nevertheless, she had replied that all but two of the waiting couples had called and been there before him.

His stomach rumbled again. Waiting at a restaurant for over an hour for a table was something he had never done. His gaze continued to dart over to the nearby taco stand, which was now closing up for the night.

Billy Jo smacked his arm. "Okay, two more are leaving their tables. Come on, hurry up, people." She tapped his arm again. She was staring through the big picture window, nothing discreet about her.

"You sure they're not leaving because of the way you're staring them down, making them feel as if you're about to walk in there, rip their plates away, and tell them they're done?"

She made a rude noise.

He took in her impatience, the way she fidgeted. She looked rather nice tonight. Her clothes were unlike the baggy things she normally wore. Girly was one thing Billy Jo wasn't, but tonight was different. He found himself really taking in everything about her, though there was nothing flirty or teasing there.

What was wrong with him? He seemed to always be drawn to the wrong kind of girl. But then, he trusted Billy Jo more than anyone. He pulled his hand over his face, wondering why he wasn't like his brothers.

"Yup...yup," she said. "Look, that's our table, and we're taking it. Come on, get up." She kept tapping his arm.

For a moment, as he took in her impatience, he thought she might even go in and yell at them to hurry up and pay the bill. "You know, just saying, that could have been us. We could have already had dinner and been on our way, but no. You insisted I make everyone feel uncomfortable and go to the back of the line because…"

"Oh, stop it, already. If you'd actually called and made a reservation earlier today like you were supposed to, we wouldn't be sitting out here, starving. What the hell is up with some of these people, though? They've been sitting there forever, done eating yet not leaving. Those two must have been married forever, because they're just staring off into space."

The way she said it, he half expected her to walk in there and over to the people at the tables in question and tell them to leave. She was staring down with the kind of look he wouldn't want to have been on the receiving end of. Complicated, difficult. Being with her was just like treading over a minefield.

He stood up beside her as she stared through the big window, leaning in.

"Could someone get up any slower?" she said. "Come on, people. Move it, already." She clapped her hands this time.

He wondered whether people could hear her from inside.

"Let's go. We're taking that table." She gestured sharply as she strode to the door and pulled it open, and he had no choice but to follow her. He gripped the edge of the door, looking right and left, really taking his time. She was already up in front of the hostess, gesturing quite sharply. Would that hostess ever forget them? Likely not.

Two couples walked out past him as he carefully took a step inside, looking around.

"Come on, Mark. Let's go," Billy Jo called out.

The hostess already had two menus in her hand, and she led them into the open restaurant, which had about twenty tables. It was well lit, with lots of windows that offered an amazing view of the now darkening sky.

"I have a window seat here," the hostess said. "Can I get you two anything to drink to start?"

Mark reached for the chair at the table for two,

which had just been cleared and wiped down but was not yet set for anyone, and pulled it out. "I'll have a pint of your lager on tap."

Billy Jo was still standing, her hands resting on the back of her chair. "A glass of your house red," she said.

The hostess left the menus on the table and walked away. Billy Jo was still standing there, not sitting, and Mark didn't have a clue what she was doing.

"You're not seriously expecting me to pull your chair out for you?" he said.

She shot him a look that told him to drop dead, a look she'd mastered, and then looped her purse over the back of the chair before pulling it out. "Don't be an ass," she said as she sat, then nodded behind him. "You have any idea who those people are over there?"

He glanced around to where she was gesturing, seeing a restaurant full of people he didn't really know.

She wiped her hands over the damp table and then rubbed them together. "Don't look," she hissed under her breath.

He turned back to her and wanted to point out how ridiculous she sounded. "You asked me if I knew who they were. If I can't look, then how am I supposed to tell you?"

One of the servers brought a basket of breadsticks along with two rolled napkins with utensils. Not exactly Mexican, but hungry was hungry. Mark reached for one and took a bite.

"Do it conspicuously," she said. "Come on. You're a cop. You should know how to watch people without them knowing you're looking at them." She was serious.

He reached for the menu and leaned on the table before glancing behind him. Then he looked back to see her standing. "No idea who you're talking about. What are you doing? I thought you were hungry." He gestured to her chair.

She reached for her purse, not pulling her eyes from his. He could see the edge to her, which was always there. "Table of four women who've been watching us, or rather you, since we walked in here. But even earlier, when we were sitting outside, they kept looking over." She leaned in again. "Come on, Mark. The table of four women at two o'clock? Please tell me they aren't women you dated and have forgotten about?"

Now he had even less interest in looking. "Okay, you know what?" he said. "I'm hungry. If they want to look, let them. And, for the record, I remember every woman I've dated. What are you doing?"

She was now standing, her bag over her shoulder. "I have to go to the bathroom. Order something to start while I'm gone," she said, then started to the back of the restaurant.

He just shook his head. Being with Billy Jo was anything but easy. He stared at the menu, the choices, as a lanky server wearing a black shirt and pants appeared with Billy Jo's wine and his beer.

"Do you have any starters before we order?" Mark said. "Chips, salsa…?" He looked up to the waiter as he took in the menu, which had so many options.

"Sure. I can bring you a basket of chips and salsa, or we have nachos with shrimp con queso." He pointed at the long list.

Mark didn't have a clue what Billy Jo wanted. "You know what? You choose," he said.

"Hi, Mark. I thought that was you," said a woman behind the waiter. She was attractive, leggy, slender, wearing a hat over a mix of dark and light hair. "I guess you don't remember meeting. I'm a friend of Sybil Gillespie. We met at the coffeehouse when she was closing up a while back." Her smile was perfect.

He could feel the unease, a knot in his stomach. He looked up to the waiter, who was still standing there, and said, "Whatever you bring is fine."

The waiter had been staring at the woman, whom Mark didn't remember meeting. "Okay then…" was all he said before he left.

Mark leaned back, wondering why the woman was smiling down at him. He took in the perfect smile of someone who seemed too familiar with him, and he wondered whether this was where he was supposed to ask how Sybil was.

"Sorry, your name is?" He gestured toward her.

She shrugged. She wore skin-tight jeans, a crop top, and a jean jacket, with heavy eyeliner and hoops in her ears. He was pretty good with faces and names, so he didn't know why he didn't remember. He thought of Sybil, super hot, exactly the type he gravitated to. Yet he hadn't stepped back in that coffeehouse since things went sideways.

"Lynn," she said. "So you don't remember me?"

He pulled in a breath, wondering what it was about the way she was staring down at him, watching him. "Sorry, I meet a lot of people. You're having dinner here with friends?"

He wondered now whether that was who Billy Jo had meant, the people watching him. He found himself glancing back over his shoulder to see the three other women, who smiled and waved. He didn't have a clue who they were—young, attractive, exactly the type that was unhealthy for him.

"Yeah, just over there," Lynn said. "We saw you walk in with that social worker, and I thought I'd come over and say hi. Sybil was just mentioning you the other day, oh so cool and forever single. She didn't mention you were seeing someone else…"

He reached for his beer and took a swallow. Something about this seemed too familiar, playing games, dancing around subjects, women sticking their noses in his business. "Well, again, Lynn, sorry I didn't remember you, but enjoy your dinner."

She hesitated, as he'd made it clear they were done, before saying, "Sure, sorry. Great to see you again, Mark. I'll let Sybil know you said hi."

He didn't pull his gaze from her as he shook his head and settled his beer down on the table, not even trying to stop the rough laugh that slipped out. He hated these games. "Please don't, Lynn. Not sure what this is, coming over here. I'm sorry I don't remember meeting you, but I'm having dinner with a friend. Whatever has you walking over here and getting in my business…"

"Oh, no," she said, cutting him off, a hint of pink in her cheeks. "I hope you didn't think that's why I came over. Of course not. I just… Well, this is embarrassing now. That's not what I meant. It was just careless small talk, really. I'm just…"

He could see how flustered she was, yet he didn't know why she was still standing there. She took two steps to Billy Jo's chair, pulled it out, and sat down. He wondered whether his eyes bugged out.

"What are you doing?"

"Look, one thing Sybil always said about you was

that you're a great guy and you'd be her first call if she was in trouble, even though things aren't good between you. Mark is who you call if you're in trouble, she said."

Something about the way she was talking had him glancing over to the back of the restaurant where Billy Jo had gone. He still didn't see her. "What's going on? Are you in trouble or something?"

She hunched a bit and leaned on the table, moving the wrapped cutlery to the side. She looked away. "Look, before you came to the island, people knew not to bother calling the police if something happened. Depending on who you were, it wouldn't be taken seriously. But Sybil said you wouldn't look away if someone you knew did something. She said you'd actually look into it and do something rather than protect someone because he was family or a friend. Is that true?"

He felt uneasy, taking in her ball cap and wondering if that was her way of hiding. "Why don't you just get to the point, Lynn? Did something happen?"

She firmed her lips and fisted her hands on the table as she sat back, looking around, then lifted her hand to the side of her head as if she didn't want anyone to see her. "Look, there's a man who comes into the coffeehouse and makes her uncomfortable. The way he looks at her, the way he acts… She took it to the chief once, but he wouldn't do anything about it."

He let out a sigh and leaned forward. "Did he do something to her? I'm kind of at a loss here. Is it just that she's uncomfortable, or is it something more? Has he threatened her in any way? Is he harassing her? You need to be a little more specific. Does she have reason to believe he'll hurt her? Who is this, anyway?"

"Look, it's not what he says but what he does, the

way he ogles her. She says it's creepy. He hasn't exactly asked her out, but he takes things as if he has every right, little things, like he helps himself to a cookie and doesn't pay for it. The last time he came in… You know that basket of muffins she keeps by the register? She went to move it, and he grabbed her arm so hard he left marks. I told her to report him, but she already did twice, before you came to the island, and all the chief said was that he'd talk to him."

"So why is it that you are coming to me and not Sybil?"

She stood up from her chair and pressed her hands to the table. "Because she said things ended badly between the two of you, and I know she's super hurt that you're interested in someone else. Call it ego, call it whatever. But the fact is that the last time she talked to the chief, the guy walked back into the café the next day, lifted the glass lid off the cake plate, and dropped it so it shattered right beside him. He didn't look away from her. All he said was oops, then told her not to take it to the chief next time she had an issue with him.

"Then he walked behind the counter, helped himself to a sandwich, and took a bite out of it before dropping it on the floor too. Of course, no one was there. Yesterday, when I stopped in, she said she wanted it to stop. He doesn't take anything worth more than a few dollars. But the fact is that he's Roland Shephard—you know, the chief's brother? I told her to call you regardless of what happened between the two of you. She just wants him to stop coming in and knows the chief won't do anything."

The last thing he wanted was to be dragged back into Sybil's world, but if someone was harassing her, he wouldn't look away. The chief's brother? "Okay, I'll talk to her," he said.

This time, Lynn didn't pull her gaze, her light brown eyes. She gave him a smile and rested her hand on his shoulder. "That's great. There. I guess that wasn't so hard after all." Then she pulled her hand away and walked off just as the waiter reappeared with a platter of steaming cheese-covered nachos.

Still no sign of Billy Jo.

What was it with women and bathrooms?

Chapter 3

As she washed her hands, Billy Jo took in the woman at the other sink, who wore a baby blue bandana around her dark hair as if to contain it. She had a round dark face and was wiping mascara that had flaked under her eyes.

Billy Jo didn't have to fix anything on her makeup-free face except for the freckles over her nose and cheeks, which she had always wished would disappear.

"You're that social worker, right?" the woman said.

Billy Jo rinsed the soap from her hands and turned her head, unsure what was coming next, knowing she'd never seen the woman before. "I am a social worker. Have we met?" She turned off the water and reached for a paper towel to dry her hands.

"No, we haven't met, but I know who you are. Saw you're friends with that detective who also showed up on the island. I know there was talk when you showed up not long after one another, coming into a new place. You're not part of the community, and that worried a lot of folks who said you'd change things in a way that would upset people. You know how it's always been done here."

Billy Jo didn't have a clue what to say. The woman stood about five inches taller than her and appeared her mom's age. She knew well that change was something no one welcomed, even if it meant something better. "I guess that's the thing about small communities. When you're new, people don't have any idea whether you'll fit in or you're some wildcard, coming in with crazy ideas to change the way things are done. I've heard it before. But hey, as you put it, I'm just a social worker."

Then there was Mark, but she wasn't talking for him. Billy Jo tossed the paper towel in the trash and lifted her bag over her shoulder, taking a step to the door.

"You know, that's the thing about someone new coming in. That person doesn't know about some of the things that go on in a community, and most times they don't want to know. For example, there are problems happening right under the nose of the chief of police."

Her hand had been on the handle of the door, but she froze, realizing this wasn't just a friendly chat. She turned back to the woman, who was now watching her in a way that said she had something on her mind. Maybe Billy Jo didn't want to know.

"Sounds like you're hinting at something," she said. "You know the chief?"

Billy Jo slid her hand over the strap of her baggy cloth purse, holding on to it over her shoulder. The woman wasn't smiling, and Billy Jo still didn't have a clue who she was.

"Everyone on the island knows the chief—or knows about him, his family, how he runs things. You kind of have to get used to it. Someone like that, with how deep his roots go here… The thing about communities is that everyone has ties going way back, and there's always one family that runs things as if they founded the place. It morphs into their kingdom, their rules. They get their hooks into the island, and it's impossible to ever get them out. It's passed down through families, and if you're part of that group, you know, and you're good with it because it benefits you.

"Most people know this, and no one ever thinks it's a problem, or if they do, they only laugh it off as if that's just the way it is. Don't know how to fix it or change it, because you learn to either put up or move on out. Everyone else just goes along and decides it's not a problem because it doesn't affect them, or that's how it's always been done. People tell you to leave it alone because it happens everywhere."

The way this woman was hinting at something only added to the giant unease Billy Jo felt, which she figured had always been with her. She'd grown up on the wrong side, it seemed, of everything. "You know, I haven't been here that long, you're right, and you evidently already know that," Billy Jo said. "But I get the sense that you know something and don't really want to say what it is. I can't help wondering if you're trying to figure out what side of the fence I'm on. Are you wondering if what you tell me will get back to the chief? I wish you would just say it. But I'm at a loss because you know who I am but I don't know who you are."

The woman reached for her small black bag and looped its gold chain over her arm before smoothing down her blue and white shirt, a little long and baggy in the front. "You know why people don't come forward when something bad has happened to them or someone they know? Because they know nothing will change. Or, worse, if they do say something, they're suddenly the one with a target on them, the one in the spotlight, with bad things happening to them, because no one ever likes the person who blows the whistle.

"And what happens to that person who calls out a liar or a thief, someone who does bad things and gets away with it? That person suddenly finds herself hunted, with her life upended and a spotlight shining down on her and her family. Skeletons she doesn't even know she had are dug up. Then she loses her job, or her friends suddenly turn away, or she has even bigger problems. Going after a cop, especially one who runs a community, is a surefire way to find yourself under investigation for something. Then your friends are either running the other way or throwing you under the bus to save their own skin."

She knew she was frowning, and she realized now what she was seeing on the woman's face and hearing in her voice. "Are you trying to figure out if I'm going to share whatever you tell me? I can assure you I won't, but then again, you don't know me. I can see you're likely trying to figure out whether you should tell me whatever it is. First, I don't know your name, because you haven't told me, so whatever you tell me isn't going to come back on you since I don't know who you are. And I get having trust issues…" She made herself stop talking. Convincing someone to trust her was something she would never try to do. She let go of the strap of her purse and lifted both her hands to stop herself. "You keep hinting at the chief, at the idea that he did something. Let's say he did. Is this something he did to you?"

The woman pursed her lips as if considering her answer. "Not to me but to someone else. As I said, it was something that was happening right under the watch of the chief, right in his own family. You know what I mean? How often do families protect their own, look the other way, or maybe wear blinders because they don't want to know the truth even though they really do? How often do you really not know that someone in your family is doing bad things to another family member? Think about it. What would you do if you found out something like that about the chief and his family?"

Billy Jo pulled her arms across her chest. She had an unsettled feeling every time she had to be around the chief, talk to him, or listen to him talk down to her as if she were less than him. Maybe that was why she'd never give him the benefit of the doubt.

"You're saying you know something about the chief, or is it someone in his family? You want to know what I'll do? Well, I won't walk into his office and tell him, if that's what you're thinking. I do know enough about him to understand that nothing goes down on this island without him knowing about it, though. I guess I would have to consider what it is and then figure out a way to handle it. But I wouldn't confront him, not someone like him."

The woman seemed to consider her reply, then nodded. "Well, you're right about one thing: You don't know me. You know how big the chief's family is?"

What did Billy Jo really know about the chief? That he was married to Gail, for one, and she'd seen photos of their grown kids, but other than that, she knew nothing. "I know very little, but maybe that's a good thing."

"The chief and his wife have a large family, with

nine siblings between them. Five are married, and three are currently single. One's been married four times. The chief has dozens of nieces and nephews and four of his own kids, three with Gail and the eldest with a woman he was married to for five minutes. Most of their family lives somewhere else, another state, another country, but there are more than a dozen of the shirttail kind who still live here.

"One of them is a niece by the name of Cheyenne Potter, just one of a few who were preyed on by someone they should've been able to trust. It started when she was fourteen, and she told her mother when she was fifteen. The predator is a man who's been married too many times and is known for his affairs. He shows up for every family dinner, gathering, or reunion. He's the one who never forgets the kids' birthdays, who puts the party hat on and gets down on a level with the little ones. He treats the boys like gold, and he loves the girls who sit on his lap… You have any idea where I'm going with this?"

She did, which was maybe the reason for the sick lump sitting heavy in her throat. She forced herself to swallow. "You're saying she was molested. How old is she? Who did it?"

"She's too old for you to do anything now. She's twenty-six. Just ended her engagement because that kind of thing messes with you and takes away any chance of having something normal. She never told her fiancé, because who in her right mind would want to talk about something like that?"

"And she didn't report it? Her mother didn't?"

The woman shook her head. "You haven't listened to anything I've said. He's family, the chief's family. You think they don't know? The funny thing too is that Cheyenne's schooling was paid for, but she dropped out and never finished her degree. She was in Boston, a long way from here, and she should've stayed there. But for some reason, she came back, and the only thing I do know is that she's not allowed to talk about it, any of it —whatever that means. She just bought a house, though where she got the money…"

The woman shrugged. "So I'm going to walk out of here now. Please don't follow me, but if the stories and rumors on this island about you are true, then I expect you'll look into it, that you won't give the chief and his family a pass just like everyone else does. Oh, and if you come looking for me, I'll deny we had this conversation. Remember, Cheyenne Potter. And if you talk to her, don't tell her where you heard this from."

The woman walked around Billy Jo and pulled open the bathroom door, leaving her standing there, pulling in a breath, feeling as if a little bomb had been dropped. She stepped out of the bathroom into a half-empty restaurant and found herself looking around for the woman, her heart pounding. But she must have already walked out. For a moment, she wondered who else knew.

She dragged her gaze over to Mark, who was sitting at the table by the window, eating what looked to be nachos. She crossed the restaurant and took in the way he lounged in the chair, those blue eyes flickering with what she thought was annoyance.

"Took you long enough," he said. "Was starting to think you ran out the back door. The waiter said the kitchen was about to close up for the night, so I overstepped and ordered you the special, a shrimp enchilada. Don't be pissed if it's not what you wanted."

"That's fine," she snapped as she flicked her hand to him, looped her purse over the back of her chair, and scraped back her chair and sat down. She glanced at the empty tables around them and leaned forward, keeping her voice down as she said, "I was just cornered in the bathroom by a woman who told me something about the chief." She scooted her chair closer, her arms resting now on the table, and glanced around. She could see she had all his attention.

Mark stilled, having just shoved a nacho into his mouth. "Is this something I'm going to want to hear?" He wiped his hands and glanced over his shoulder before settling those baby blue eyes on her.

She pulled in a breath. "Probably not, but let me ask you this: What do you know about the chief's family? Would he cover up a crime to protect a relative?"

Mark glanced to the side again and then behind him as if to make sure no one was listening. "I think you'd better tell me what this woman said to you," he said, an edge to his voice. "And, Billy Jo, don't leave anything out."

Chapter 4

Mark took in Gail, who was rustling papers, stapling something, then slid around in his chair and took in the chief. The man was in his office, talking on the phone. Mark's dog was lying on the dog bed, his eyes open, staring at him.

His phone dinged with another message from Billy Jo:

Well?

So much for their peaceful dinner out. The evening had turned into a bombshell of secrets about the chief's family.

He turned off the screen and turned his phone over, still trying to get his head around what Billy Jo had told him. Then there was Sybil at the coffee shop. He planned to stop in later and have a talk about Roland Shephard, who was harassing her. But as he stared at Gail, he had no clue how to go about tactfully and carefully looking into the problem in the chief's family without the chief and her knowing.

What was the story, the real story?

"What's on your mind, Mark?"

He only lifted his gaze from where he lounged in his chair, giving his head a shake, not missing the way Gail seemed to be studying him with an amused grin. He really did like her and the way she served as a buffer between him and the chief.

"Quiet day on the island," she said, teasing. "You sure there isn't something?"

"Nope, just waiting for the phone to ring and enjoying the peace and quiet for a moment without having to handle some problem," he replied. Then he heard the ding of his phone again, and he noticed the interest in Gail's expression.

"Someone seems persistent," she said.

He took in the long line of texts from Billy Jo:

Did you ask?

Why aren't you answering?

I've done my part. No report here.

???

He lifted his gaze to the ceiling and texted back: *Not yet. Give me a minute.*

He knew Billy Jo wanted him to get the inside scoop on who this Cheyenne Potter was and whether she was related to the chief or Gail.

Then there was Sybil. He hadn't shared the other problem in the chief's family with Billy Jo. Was it the same person?

"Yeah, just a friend, you know," he said. He didn't know what to make of the way Gail smirked.

"I heard you and Billy Jo tried out the new Mexican restaurant last night. Also heard you had to wait after showing up and making Lindy, who was hostessing last night, put you at the bottom of the list even though she had a table ready for you."

"You spying on me, Gail?" he said. There was something about this place. It seemed every move he made was reported back to Gail, the chief, and everyone else in town. It was the kind of thing that made him really uneasy. He gestured vaguely when she quirked a brow. "Billy Jo pointed out to me that I'd used my position as a cop to get to the front of the line, and that kind of abuse of authority is a problem."

Gail let out a sharp laugh. "Oh, I see. She's really got you toeing the line. Man, I love that girl."

He didn't know what to make of that comment, considering he had a mind of his own but just didn't see things the way Billy Jo did. "I'm not toeing anything. I just didn't believe her. When I asked the hostess last night whether she'd put me at the top of the list and given me a table over everyone who was already waiting or had called to reserve, I didn't expect her to say yes. So it's not about toeing the line. It's about the fact that I didn't even realize it was happening."

She pulled in a sharp breath, watching him. "You know, Mark, I remember years ago, when I still worked in the male-dominated banking industry, all the men I worked with—or rather, under—walked right through the doors that were open wide to them. They didn't see the struggles I had, being a woman, or the struggles others had because they weren't white. The men I worked with landed so easily into positions of power because of who they were and how they looked. They didn't see all the hurdles I had jumped through to get the position I had, from delivering them their coffee, to picking up their mail, to dry cleaning their suits, to even dusting down their desks only to be left in the office when the boys all gathered at the club for drinks.

"Don't get me wrong; they were friendly, even nice. They told me hello, asked how my night was. But I was not on their level, and the worst thing was that they never even saw that. It was clear from simple things, such as a favorite table always waiting for them at a restaurant when everyone else was put on a list and had to wait. Honestly, I remember bringing it up once to this man we'll call Fred, and the look he gave me, it was as if I'd lost my mind.

"That told me everything. He didn't believe he was getting anything special, said I was being overdramatic. Yet he could pick up the phone and call anyone, a lawyer, another bank, some retail giant, and get put right through to the corporate president. You know what really got me was the fact that it was people like him who were the gatekeepers, and the people who work in those places simply conform—like the girl who works a minimum-wage job and had your table ready because she was conditioned to automatically give you a leg up because of your power, your position."

Mark hadn't realized he was squeezing his phone. He set it down. He hadn't expected this, not from Gail. "So, what, are you saying I'm at fault here? Geez, you sound like Billy Jo..." He sat forward. Damn, he felt uncomfortable, and he didn't understand how he hadn't seen what she was talking about.

"Oh, don't get your panties in a knot, Mark. It's how this country was built. You can't change centuries of how things have been done overnight. People aren't ready for the kind of change that needs to happen. People, even minorities, keep doing the same old thing even if it doesn't work just because it's familiar. Something new is uncomfortable, and no one likes that. Just mentioning change is enough to start a fight. That's not your fault. But if you don't turn around and see what's happening to the person behind you who doesn't look like you, that's on you."

He gestured toward her. "You're making it sound as if it's up to me to fix this."

She stood up and stacked her files. The way she looked over to him, for a moment she seemed so much like his mom, ready to set him straight. "It is up to you, Mark. It's up to every white male out there who looks like you to stop in that doorway, when something is so easy for you that you don't even realize it, and turn around. It's up to you to ask if you got a job fairly, if you're making more money because you're white and male, if you have the ability to call anyone and go over the heads of people everyone else has to deal with, people who don't get the same service as you, the same benefit as you. You thought it was a simple dinner out?" she added in a teasing tone.

He found himself looking over to Carmen's empty desk. "Do I make more money than Carmen?" he said, his heart thudding. He just assumed…what, that it didn't matter?

Gail pulled in a breath and let it out. "She's not a detective. You are," was all she said.

He dragged his gaze from Gail back to the empty desk, thinking of the prickly deputy who always had his back. He knew what Gail hadn't come right out and said. "But she does the same job as I do."

Gail pulled open the filing cabinet and started tucking in her files as he sat there at his desk, unable to figure out why he was so uncomfortable. "How about that, Mark? Good on you for noticing. She does do the same job, but she's not a detective. Her title is deputy, which is a way of justifying the wage difference. It comes down from the top, the state, all the way to the county, the mayor, and the council. Even though we don't have a sea of white men running everything like we once did, we do have minorities who have moved into those positions and conform, carrying on the same way of doing things. So no, Carmen doesn't get paid what you do. You technically have more authority than she does, although, job to job, what you do here on this island is exactly the same. The only difference is that you have a title, and she doesn't."

How the hell had they gone so far down this rabbit hole? He had to remind himself to blink, to pull in a breath. "This isn't okay," he replied. He didn't know what else to say.

"No, it's not, Mark."

"Isn't the head of the town council a woman?" He was sure of that.

Gail rested her hand on the files in the cabinet. "Did you miss the part about conforming? To be clear, Mary Jane Trundell faced the same closed doors I did, watching as promotions she would've earned were given to men who had no qualifications. She was called honey, fetched coffee, made less than her male coworkers, and had to claw her way to where she is. Yet she was all for the idea of a white male being the detective with higher pay. She argued that Carmen could not have a promotion, so, as a result, the title of deputy earns her twenty percent less. Kind of leaves you with a warm and fuzzy feeling, doesn't it?"

From the way Gail shoved the filing cabinet closed, he wasn't sure whether she was angry and finished making her point or whether she still had something else to point out about how he didn't see what was happening around him.

"I swear, Mark, this is the first time I've seen you at such a loss for what to say," she said. "But, as I said, I think Billy Jo is good for you. Glad to hear you two are seeing each other."

"Billy Jo and I are just friends, Gail…"

Good friends, and she was the one person he found himself wanting to talk to about anything and everything—except Sybil.

"Oh, please," Gail said. "Next you'll be telling me you're seeing someone else or that Billy Jo is. Bite the bullet, Mark. Make it official. You're perfect for each other. In fact, why don't you bring her for dinner tonight at the house?"

His phone dinged again, but he didn't turn it over. Gail was walking over to the coffeemaker and pulling out the basket of grounds—to make a pot for him?

He pushed back his chair and stood up. "You know what, Gail? Let me make the coffee," he said, shrugging out of his jean jacket and tossing it over the back of his chair.

She turned around, holding the basket, confusion knitting her brows. "You want to make coffee?"

He reached to take the basket of grounds from her. "I don't want you waiting on me. I can make coffee. I mean, you just finished pointing out how I don't see things."

She was still gripping the basket. He wondered if she'd refuse. When she relented, he wasn't sure whether he saw panic or distrust in her expression. "Just make sure you wipe up the grounds you spill on the counter, only fill it half full, use cold water to fill the carafe, and…"

"Do you want to make it?"

She ripped the basket from his hands. "I don't want to clean up a mess, and I want it done the right way."

He said nothing, wondering if he should point out that he'd offered.

"Don't say it," she snapped.

"Say what? All I was going to say is that Billy Jo and I would love to come for dinner. So what time should we be there?"

They could talk about family, the personal kind of stuff they didn't talk about at work, and Billy Jo wouldn't be texting him about it every five minutes.

Gail filled the carafe with water. "Come about six."

He heard the ding of his phone again and started back to his desk. As he did, the chief stepped out of his office and said something to Gail in a low voice. Gail was a complicated woman, and her husband was a man Mark would always keep an eye on.

He picked up his phone and saw another message from Billy Jo:

Hello, what are you doing?

He replied, *Got us an invite to dinner at the chief and Gail's tonight.*

He spotted three dots, then nothing. Then a thumbs-up appeared.

Okay, one woman appeased. Now he had to figure out how he was going to find out everything he could about Cheyenne Potter before dinner that night. Then there was Sybil. He needed to find her and have a talk with her about this nuisance brother of the chief.

He dragged his hand over his face, knowing he was being dragged deeper into something that could end badly for him and his career as a cop.

Chapter 5

Mark had been unusually quiet since pulling in to pick her up five minutes after she got home. He'd blasted the horn without getting out of his Jeep, which she knew was his way of saying, "I'm here. Let's go—and hurry up about it!"

At any other time, she'd likely have ignored him, but as he sat in his idling Jeep, Lucky panting in the back seat, the floor of the passenger side free of takeout packaging, something about Mark just seemed off.

"So how did you manage to get us invited for dinner at the chief's?" she said as he backed out and swung around, already shifting gears while driving out to the road. She couldn't see his eyes behind the dark sunglasses he always wore when driving, but she could sense an edge to him tonight.

"I didn't. Gail suggested it as I was warding off all your texts, trying to figure out a way to find out who Cheyenne Potter is, considering she didn't show up in the database. I figured a nice social get-together away from the office would be the perfect spot to talk about family." He glanced over to her and then back to the road.

Lucky leaned forward and licked her face, and she reached back and rubbed his head, his floppy ears. She really loved Mark's dog.

"Well, I did Google Cheyenne," Billy Jo said. "She's on social media, with all kinds of photos with friends, selfies. Pretty girl, but no privacy settings. From what I can see, she loves to play some Candy Crush game and hasn't figured out that her online profile shows everywhere she goes and everything she does. If I ever try to sign up for one, remind me why it's a good idea to keep things offline."

He only shook his head. She'd expected a smile, but there was nothing. Okay, something was up.

"Anyway, I did cover the bases on my end and search the DCFS records, but her name never came up. So what's the plan tonight? How are you going to bring up Cheyenne and steer the conversation there?"

He darted his gaze to her and back to the road, and she could tell how off he was by the frown he couldn't hide. "I'm not planning on bringing it up. That's why you're here to help steer the conversation to family. You said she's a niece? So find out the details of their family without asking outright. You know this could be some wild goose chase or someone messing with you. You said you didn't know who this woman was, that she wouldn't give her name but she knew you and me. This could be nothing except someone trying to stir something up and have us walking into a problem with the chief and Gail."

That wasn't what she'd expected from him.

"Everything okay there, Mark? You seem not your cheerful self."

He rolled his shoulders the way she knew he did when he felt cornered, then let out a heavy sigh. "This isn't a walk in the park, you know. I'm already on the wrong side of the chief, but I like Gail, so I'm having a hard time with the idea that she could know about this, if it's true. You said Cheyenne Potter told her mother, but nothing happened. Would her mother have told Gail and the chief? If they weren't all over this, I don't understand. It makes no sense. Family doesn't do that, none that I know of. There has to be more to it, or someone's created a story to stir things up."

She didn't pull her gaze from him. She could see how much trouble he was having with the idea as he pulled into a driveway that led up to a two-story house on twenty acres that belonged to the chief. It was impressive, and she knew it had been in the family a long time.

Mark parked beside the police cruiser and Gail's white Tundra, and Billy Jo put her hand on the door as he turned off the engine.

"You know, Mark, I get that you're having trouble with this, but the thing about families is that you don't really know what goes on behind closed doors. The picture you see from the outside is what the family wants you to see so you would never believe the ugly truth." She yanked the door open.

Mark sighed heavily and ran his hand roughly over the top of his head. "You think I don't know that? I do." He gestured sharply. "I'm just saying in this, it doesn't make sense. So how about we don't crucify this family and convict them because of something that hasn't even been substantiated? And especially not with this kind of accusation, because if we sound the alarm and it's found to be untrue, you can't un-ring the bell. The damage is done, and you've already destroyed someone's life." He dragged his sunglasses off.

The strength that seemed to radiate from his expression was mixed with something she had never seen before, and she realized she couldn't push him tonight. Something was up.

She only shrugged as she stepped out. Mark already had the dog out, and Lucky trotted all the way to the open front door, in which the chief was standing.

The man gave all his attention to Lucky, leaning over and patting him, running his hand over his ears. "Lucky, come on in here. Gail has a big old bone ready for you."

Billy Jo didn't miss the fondness he seemed to have for the dog, who was first in the house, walking in as if he were an invited guest. She kept her gaze on a moody Mark as they walked around the front of the Jeep.

"Mark," the chief said, nodding to him.

For a second, from the look that lingered between the two of them, she suspected things were already quickly going sideways. Then the chief dragged his unsmiling gaze over to her.

"Billy Jo, glad you could come," he said. He gestured wide, sweeping to the open door for them to come in.

She could hear Gail making a fuss over the dog, who apparently knew exactly where to go, as she went in first, Mark behind her. She slipped off her flats, noting that Mark only wiped off his cowboy boots before gesturing for her to keep going.

The chief closed the door behind them, and they headed into the kitchen, which was big and open to the family room and a deck out back, where, through the open sliding glass door, she could see a barbecue smoking.

"Hey there, Billy Jo," Gail said. "It's great to see the two of you. Wine, right? Red?"

So she'd remembered.

"Sure, thank you," Billy Jo said as she pulled out a high-back padded stool at the island. She felt Mark's hand settle on the back of it as she sat down.

Gail handed him a cold beer from the fridge and poured red wine in a glass for Billy Jo, who took in the salad Gail was making and a plate of burger patties ready to go on the grill.

"So nice to see the two of you together and catch up away from work," Gail continued. "So how have things been with DCFS, Billy Jo? Heard from Tolly that you all had an issue last week removing a young boy from his home."

Right, the new policy had her being accompanied by the police to any incident now, and the chief had been the one who got that call.

"Nothing unusual, just the same distressing call, having to pull a child from the only home he's known and stick him with a bunch of strangers."

Having the chief there had only added to the anxiety. The child had been terrified, the mother distraught, but their life was now just notes in a file.

"I noticed your family portrait above the fireplace over there," Billy Jo said. "Your kids? I don't remember hearing if they live here on the island."

Mark was leaning on the island beside her, so close, and she knew he was letting her take the lead on this. At the same time, he had been and still was unusually quiet.

The chief reached for a beer that was already open on the counter and took a swallow, looking from her to Mark.

"Funny thing about kids," Gail said. "They leave and say they'll never come back, that they can't wait to get off this island, but Richard and Lori moved back last year. Trish is studying in Paris under a pastry chef right now, and Graham is back in Minneapolis, where his mom lives. He's Tolly's son, from his first wife. What is he doing now, Tolly?"

Billy Jo turned her head, taking in the photo and the smiling tall black kid who towered over the chief. She looked back to him, noting that he hadn't pulled his gaze.

The chief shrugged. "Mechanics. Has an uncle there who took him under his wing."

She didn't know what to make of that comment. Just then, the dog strode back in the open door, his tongue hanging out, and headed to a bowl of water on the floor, which he lapped up.

"Tolly, grab that bone in the fridge and take it out on the back deck to give to Lucky," said Gail.

There was something about the way the chief seemed to follow her orders. Billy Jo watched as he pulled open the fridge and pulled out a prime rib bone on a plate.

"Come on there, Lucky," he said, and the dog followed.

Mark seemed to track the chief, and she elbowed him sharply when Gail turned away. She made a face when he frowned down at her.

"So how long have you lived here on this island?" she asked.

Gail opened the fridge, pulled out a potato salad, and rested it on the long granite counter. The center island had a gas insert, and it appeared the place had been freshly remodeled. "Oh, I grew up here, just like Tolly did. It's home. The place is in the blood. Can't imagine living anywhere else. Did at one time in my younger corporate life, but I moved back here when Tolly and I got married. So what about you and Mark? Are you both finding that this island life is growing on you? It's a great place to raise kids."

Billy Jo reached for her wine, lifted the glass, and took a swallow. Gail's questions were veering into that personal territory of where she and Mark were or were not. She dragged her gaze to Mark, who still hadn't said anything, and she wasn't sure what to make of the way he was watching her. "It's good here, right, Mark?"

He pulled in a breath. "Yup. You want those burgers on the grill?" He gestured to the plate.

Gail reached for it and handed it to him. "Yeah, good idea. Take this out to Tolly and tell him to get them started."

Mark headed out the back door, where the chief was watching the dog, who was now lying on the deck, chomping on the bone.

"Everything okay between you two?" Gail said.

It took Billy Jo a second to realize the woman had picked up on something. She just took in the chief and Mark, the barbecue now open. The two seemed to be talking. "Yeah, it's just Mark, you know, moody. Figure he had a rough day. He tends to clam up."

The smile and soft chuckle from Gail had her really looking at the woman as she said, "Ah. I gave him a little bit of a hard time, showing him the reality of what he doesn't see. Could tell I hit a nerve. Mark doesn't hide it well when he's rattled. Tolly has warned me I tend to take it too far sometimes."

"Oh…?" She wasn't sure she should ask and hoped it wasn't about her.

"He's a good guy, though. But you know that already."

She wondered whether her face portrayed her unease. "You're right, I do know that. Considering I don't have family here, I call on Mark for anything. You and Tolly have other family here?" She wanted to pat herself on the back for her quick thinking.

"Sure we do. My two sisters are here, but my brother is down in Sacramento. Have a few nieces and nephews on my side, and Tolly has two brothers and four sisters. We had a big reunion just last year and were missing only four."

Gail stepped over to the bookshelf, which held a framed photo, and walked back over with it. It looked like forty people, easy. She held out the photo, and Billy Jo took it, her gaze seeking out Cheyenne Potter, whom she'd seen online. There she was on the end, not smiling. A man next to her had his hand on her shoulder.

"I've seen her in town. Who is this?" she said, wondering how the lie could roll off her tongue so easily as she pointed to Cheyenne in the photo.

"Oh, that's Cheyenne, my sister Patrice's daughter. She owns the nail studio down on main street. Did you have your nails done? Is that where you saw her?"

Billy Jo was still holding the photo, taking in the curiosity that lingered in the way Gail was watching her. The woman was smart. Billy Jo needed to be careful. She held up her hand and her short nails. "These?

Please. I am the last person to have my nails done. Is that her father behind her with his hand on her shoulder? And which ones are your sisters?"

Gail leaned on the counter and seemed to really look at the picture. "My sister Bev is here, and Patrice is there…" She pointed to two women in front who were sitting on the grass, laughing together, their arms linked. "That's Philip behind Cheyenne. He's married to Bev… And those are our kids, there."

Billy Jo took in the photo. The family seemed picture-perfect. But something about Philip's hand on Cheyenne's shoulder had her stomach knotting.

"Gail, burgers are almost ready…" the chief called out from where he was barbecuing, Mark beside him.

Gail reached for the framed photo. "Okay, I'll grab the buns. Billy Jo, can you take the potato salad and put it on the table?"

And that was the end of that. Gail put the photo back on the bookshelf, and Billy Jo slid off the stool. Mark walked in and over to her as she reached for the potato salad, and Gail was gone down the hallway—to a pantry, she thought.

"Well?" he said in a low voice.

"Yup. Cheyenne is the daughter of Gail's sister Patrice. There's a photo over there. And behind her is her uncle, married to her other sister," she whispered.

Gail walked back in. Mark had that way of looking at her that told her he understood what she was saying. He was so close, in her space.

"What are you two whispering about?" Gail said. "Whose place you're going to after or just plans in general?"

Mark stepped back. "You just don't let up, do you?" he said teasingly.

Gail laughed softly. "Nope, not when you two look this good together."

Mark just shook his head and stepped around her. When Billy Jo placed the potato salad on the table, she turned to see Mark already reaching for her wine on the island. The chief walked in with the plate of burgers, and Billy Jo pulled out a chair on the other side of the table, taking in the redheaded cowboy in the jean jacket he never took off, realizing she liked him more than a friend ever should.

Chapter 6

After dropping off Billy Jo, Mark didn't like the thoughts that plagued him. He knew and looked up to Gail, and he just didn't understand how the story of abuse in her family could be true. He couldn't make sense of the possibility that Gail, who was the buffer between him and the chief, could know something like that was going on right under her nose. The story couldn't be true, because it would rock not just her world but her entire family's.

He was still uneasy, too, about the way Billy Jo had been looking at him from across the table. Maybe that was why he'd dropped her off with the Jeep still running and kept the conversation focused on business, on Cheyenne Potter and the fact that Billy Jo would contact her the next day.

That was good, considering Mark needed to handle the matter of coffeehouse girl Sybil and the chief's so-called loose cannon of a brother. Those had been the chief's exact words when Mark asked him casually about Roland Shephard and why he wouldn't leave

Sybil Gillespie alone. While barbecuing, the chief had said he'd handle it and that Rolly always managed to do things that were out of character. Mark wondered whether that was the chief's way of explaining that his brother would continue to harass Sybil.

He slowed the Jeep as he drove into town and spotted the café just ahead. Sybil was stepping out, flicking off the lights, and pulling the door closed. He swung in and parked in front, seeing the second she spotted him. Her key was in the lock, her long hair pulled back. He didn't think he'd ever forget those long slender legs, her perfect body under those blue jeans and the loose cream cardigan pulled over her T-shirt.

He turned off the Jeep and opened his door, glancing back to the dog, who lifted his head. "Stay," was all he said to Lucky before he stepped out, closed the door, and took one step after the other, walking right over to Sybil, who didn't appear happy in the least to see him.

Could he blame her? Not really.

"Mark, I'm closed now," she said quite tersely.

"Not here for coffee. Here to talk to you, if you have a minute." He stopped in front of her and took in her round face, those lips he'd kissed too many times, and those eyes that flickered with an emotion he didn't want to consider too long. He glanced away and then back to her when she hadn't said anything.

She lifted her chin. "About what, Mark? As I said, I'm closed. It's been a long day, I'm tired…"

"It's about Roland Shephard." He cut her off.

Her mouth made an O, and she let out a sharp breath.

"Maybe we should talk inside," he added, as he could see her considering it.

She shoved her key back in the lock and opened the door, then stepped inside, and Mark followed her as she strode to the first table and set down her bag. He reached over and flicked on the light in the dimness, then closed the door behind him.

"So what is this about Roland Shephard? Let me guess: He's complaining about me now?" She made a rude noise.

Mark shook his head. "No, a friend of yours—Lynn, I think she said her name was? Well, she stopped by my table last night and mentioned all the trouble you've been having with the chief's brother. Said you even went to the chief about him."

"Oh, I went to him, all right, and told him to get his creepy brother to stay out of my coffeehouse. I told him his brother felt he could do anything he wanted, helping himself to anything on the counter without paying for it —a cookie, a muffin. The chief said he'd take care of it, but all that got me was an angry Roland who broke an eighty-dollar glass cake cover by dropping it on the floor. Then he helped himself to a bag of coffee and a sand-wich, which he took a bite of, dumped on the floor, and stepped on. Any idea the mess egg salad makes?"

She pulled her arms across her chest, and he could see her anger. "I knew he was pissed, and he made his point. I wasn't going to be able to stop him from tormenting me. The only thing I'm grateful for is that he hasn't run off any of my business yet. Just to be clear, he always waits for the coffeehouse to be empty, with no one watching, before he pulls this on me." She uncrossed her arms and held them straight down, fisting her hands, before tapping her chest.

Mark could see how upset she was. "Did he threaten you in any way? Your friend Lynn mentioned you haven't gone back to the chief and talked to him. You know you could always have a trespass issued against him, barring him from your premises for the next year."

She angled her head. For a moment, he thought a smile touched her lips, but there was such sadness that it didn't reach her eyes. "Look, I'm sure Lynn was trying to help, but she overstepped in coming to you, Mark. The chief already made it clear that Roland is his brother and that he'd talk to him, but that talk had Roland right back in my café, pissed, and a pissed Roland is not someone I want around me. I'm looking over my shoulder now because I don't know if he's going to be waiting for me when I walk out of the coffee shop, if he'll hurt me, or what he'll do. I mean, the way he looks at me is creepy."

She hissed and pulled in a breath. "No, I'm done going to the chief, who made it clear that these are… minor annoyances, he called them. You know the chief pulled ten dollars out of his pocket and handed it to me to pay for, as he called it, the refreshments his brother took? Ten dollars!"

He winced, then wondered if this was something the chief had always had to do, cleaning up after his brother. "You know, Sybil, there are a couple things you should do, like setting up surveillance cameras." He looked around the room.

She pulled her arms across her chest again. "And then what? You forget he's still the chief's brother. If he were anyone else, not the chief's brother, would he not have been charged?"

He didn't look away, because this wasn't the fun Sybil he was used to. Apparently, this was a side she'd hidden. He didn't know why she'd never mentioned this to him before when they were sleeping together, doing the casual fun thing. "Well, the thing is, Sybil, now I know about it. Surveillance is proof of his doing it, and if he's as smart as you're saying, if he sees the camera, he may think twice. But in the meantime, I'm serious about the trespass. I'll issue it, not the chief."

Her mouth was tight. She was uncomfortable. "And when he shows up here, furious, then what? With the chief on his side, you really think this will be anything more than just a piece of paper? I mean, I'm not a fool, Mark. There will be blowback on me."

He rested a hand on her shoulder. "I'll handle it. Step one, let's get him out of here. I'll have a word with him, and if you have any trouble, call me," he said, letting his hand drop when her gaze softened.

"All right. Issue it, then." She reached for her bag and slung it over her shoulder. "And, Mark?"

He had his hand on the door and had pulled it open as Sybil reached for the light and flicked it off. He took in the way she walked, the way she moved, the way she stopped right beside him and was so close, pressing her hand to his chest, standing in the open doorway.

"Thanks for stopping by and wanting to help me," she said. Then she rose up on her tiptoes, pressed a kiss to his cheek, and strode out of the café.

He pulled the door closed. "You're welcome, Sybil," he said.

She shoved her key in the door and locked it, and

Mark took in her small pickup parked at the side of the building as she walked over to it.

"Again, call me if he shows up," he said. "I mean as soon as he walks in, before he has a chance to do anything."

There it was, that flirty smile. She nodded. "Okay, I will, Mark," she said. Then she climbed in her little pickup and started the engine, and Mark climbed in his own Jeep and watched as Sybil flicked her hand to him in a little wave.

He took in the dog, who was now sitting up, staring at him.

"I'm not doing anything stupid," he said. "It's cop stuff, what I'd do for anyone. She's no different."

The dog whined and licked his face, and Mark scratched his chin, glancing at the seat Billy Jo had just been sitting in, wondering why he felt guilty. Maybe he should have mentioned the problems Sybil was having to her—even though this was police business. Something about seeing his ex made him feel he was wading into a situation that could end up bringing a heap of trouble down on his head.

"You're being ridiculous, Mark," he said to himself.

Sybil honked as she drove away.

"Rolly, Rolly, Rolly," he muttered as he backed out and put the Jeep in drive. "Let's have a talk, you and me. Just what do you think you're doing?"

He pictured what would happen when the chief found out. Likely, there would be fireworks, and maybe he would be one step closer to being shown the door.

He gave his head a shake as he mumbled under his breath, "You just can't help yourself, can you, Mark?"

Chapter 7

Billy Jo took in her short nails and ordinary hands as she stood in the softly lit waiting area of Nails & Glitter, a small day spa tucked between a craft shop and a specialty teahouse. She'd never been to either, which was maybe why she'd never really noticed this street at the edge of town.

Soft, relaxing music was playing low in the background. She heard footsteps and a voice from one of the rooms in back, and then an older woman with short white hair walked out with a young woman with super long dark hair.

Cheyenne. She recognized her from the photos she'd posted online.

"Is that all for you today, Mrs. Hartley?"

"Yes, Cheyenne, just the nails today. Can you book me in for the same time in two weeks? This time I promise to actually remember."

Billy Jo stood off to the side, waiting for the woman to pay. She took in the bright smile Cheyenne offered as the older woman, who had pale pink nails, held one hand up as she shoved her debit card back into the side of her bag. Billy Jo took in the shelves of polish and makeup for sale, all the girly stuff she'd never been drawn to buying.

"Thanks again, Cheyenne. See you in a few weeks." The old woman started walking to the door.

"Bye now, Mrs. Hartley," Cheyenne called out as she tucked the receipt in a drawer. Then she offered a bright smile to Billy Jo. "You're here to have your nails done?"

"Yes, I have an appointment, Billy Jo McCabe," she said, fisting the strap of her purse, watching as Cheyenne stood up. She wore a black and white sundress with flipflops, and she had a nice figure, with glitter on her nails.

"Is this your first time here?" Cheyenne said. She had a pleasing smile, and a small nose stud flickered in the light. The ends of her dark hair were dyed pink, and her makeup wasn't overly thick.

"Yeah, just thought why not have these nails looked after?"

"Well, I appreciate the business. Come on back."

Billy Jo followed Cheyenne to one of two back rooms. The door was dark wood, the carpeting light beige, and the ambiance reminded her of the kinds of spas Rose would drag her to, with faint soft music, relaxing colors on the walls. The place was the opposite of loud and busy.

She sat in a comfortable chair and took in the table between them, with a towel ready for her hands and polish at the side, the nail kit all ready.

Cheyenne had her back to her, running a tap and filling a bowl with water. "So are you just visiting the island?" she said before she turned around, carrying the plastic bowl, which had suds in it. She rested it in front of Billy Jo. "Just put your fingers in there to soak."

As Billy Jo settled her hands in the warm water, trying to see the family resemblance, Cheyenne pulled out the padded office chair opposite her. "No, I moved here a while back. I'm actually a social worker on the island."

"Okay. I'll take one of your hands now." Cheyenne reached for her hand.

She took in the rounded cheeks of a young woman who seemed just like everyone else. What exactly was she looking for? Someone who was angry, with a chip on her shoulder? Someone different?

Maybe Mark was right and the woman in the bathroom had been messing with her.

"That doesn't sound like the kind of work that would be any fun," Cheyenne said. "Why a social worker?" She flicked her blue eyes up to Billy Jo as she started pushing her cuticles back.

"Because of how I grew up. I didn't have a voice. I grew up in the system, bounced from foster home to foster home, unwanted, and had no one who really gave a damn about me. I fought off unwanted attention from foster brothers. I learned fast as a kid, knowing I couldn't tell anyone who would believe me. It became a matter of survival until my mom and dad adopted me when I was fifteen. You know, I was lucky. But those first fifteen years had decided my outcome. So yeah, social work. Not a happy job, but the problem is that those kids don't have anyone else to speak for them. So I will," she said, wondering whether Cheyenne was even listening to her as she cut her nails.

Now and then, the woman flicked up her gaze,

offering what Billy Jo thought was a practiced smile. "That sounds rough," she said. "Sorry for what you had to go through."

Okay, this was going to be harder than she'd thought.

"Do you see a lot of that kind of thing on this island?" Cheyenne asked.

She recalled the faces of the kids she'd picked up and placed, which she didn't think she'd ever get out of her mind. "It happens in the kinds of places you'd never expect. You place a kid in a home you think should be safe, with respectable people who check all the right boxes, but you never know what's really going on behind closed doors. Kids want only one thing, and that's to be loved and trusted. But most of these kids are already scarred and broken, angry. They've been severely neglected, or they have no self-esteem, and that makes them easy targets for grooming by a predator."

Cheyenne stilled for a second, then picked up the file and started filing her nails. "Are you talking about situations you've pulled kids from or places you've put them?" Her brows knit.

Billy Jo paused. She was treading a fine line. "Both, unfortunately."

"How could someone hate a little kid so much as to do that to them?" Cheyenne tsked under her breath. "Okay, put this one back in the water. Give me your other hand." Her touch was soft, and she put all her focus into cleaning up Billy Jo's nails.

"You would think that, wouldn't you? Even I did, growing up, but I learned something from all the psychology courses my dad made me take and the shrinks' sofas I had to sit on because he wanted to fix me. It wasn't about hate. As sick as it is, that abuser, that monster who preys on kids, needs that attention himself. The worst is how he goes about it, getting that kid to trust him. In foster care, you're already screwed up to begin with, with low self-esteem, just wanting love. You have bottled-up anger and hurt in your eyes. But it even happens to kids in what seem like perfect families.

"I've always wondered why one girl in a family is molested by a male relative and others aren't. It made no sense to me, but then I learned it's about more than meets the eye. Kids need someone to look up to, and predators know that. They know who to pick. They never choose the child with strong self-confidence and self-esteem. They look for the one in whose eyes they can see anger toward a parent or guardian, toward a system, or a child who wants retaliation against her parents. In families where it happens, the predator works to make that kid feel good, and if the abuser is good at that, he starts grooming."

Cheyenne gripped her hand, then let go, lifting her gaze to her slowly as she sat back. "That sounds absolutely sick."

Billy Jo angled her head. For a moment, she wondered whether she was going too far. Maybe this was some sick game on the part of a woman she didn't know. It happened. "It is," she continued, "but if parents actually paid attention to the signs and what to look for, it wouldn't happen to their kid, right under their watch. Maybe they have a party and someone is hanging around with the little kids rather than the adults, or someone gives extra to one kid, sitting her on his knee, down on the floor, cuddling, holding, hugging her."

Cheyenne firmed her lips and finished up her other hand. Something about her face told Billy Jo she'd touched on something.

"You know," Billy Jo said, "one of the things that doesn't surprise me anymore is the number of grown women this has happened to, and they've never told anyone, or if they did, they weren't believed. Or, worse, they somehow thought it was their fault, or there was something wrong with them. Some won't admit it happened because, at the time, it felt good…"

"Okay. Which color polish do you want?" Cheyenne cut her off and was out of her chair, grabbing the trolly on wheels with all the colors. "Did you want to go wild and crazy with something dark, or something lighter…?"

Billy Jo knew she was done talking. "Clear is good," she said.

The little silver bell at the front desk dinged.

"Can you excuse me for a second? I'll be right back," Cheyenne said before striding out of the room, and Billy Jo cursed the interruption as she heard a familiar voice.

"Hi there, Cheyenne. How're you doing? Was hoping you could slip me in for a quick fix-me-up. Pretty please?"

Billy Jo rolled her eyes. She would've known Sybil's voice anywhere.

"Well, I'm just finishing up with a client in back, if you want to wait," Cheyenne said. "Or you can come back, and then I can slip you in. You got a hot date or something?"

Billy Jo didn't miss the teasing and friendliness of what sounded like two women who knew each other.

"Well, I'm hoping so," Sybil said. "I never expected Mark to show up like he did last night. That man cares, and I just want to look perfect, be ready. You know when you meet that one perfect guy? Well, I think I might get that second chance."

"You're talking about that detective?"

"The hottie himself."

Billy Jo's ears were ringing as she listened to the laughter. She took in her nails, which still needed polish, but she didn't want it.

"Why don't you come back in, say, ten minutes?" Cheyenne said.

Billy Jo wiped her hands as she listened to the door, feeling an unwelcome ball of fire in her stomach that was too familiar.

Cheyenne strode back in.

"You know what, Cheyenne?" Billy Jo said. "Forget the polish. I forgot about an appointment I have, and I'm now late for it…" She made a motion of looking at her wrist and then scooted out of the chair, grabbing her bag, taking in the surprise in Cheyenne's expression.

"Are you sure? I haven't finished your nails yet. I can paint them quickly…"

Billy Jo pulled out her wallet as she strode out to the front, thankful she didn't have to face Sybil. "Don't worry about it. They'd be chipped by day's end, anyway. How much do I owe you?"

Cheyenne hurried around the desk as Billy Jo pulled out her debit card. "Thirty-eight, but since I didn't add polish…"

Billy Jo waved her hand. "Thirty-eight is good," she said, then tapped her card on the debit machine, waved off the receipt, and tucked her wallet back in her purse before hurrying out the door.

As she closed the door behind her, she let out a breath, picturing that rugged arrogant redheaded asshole, too good looking for his own good, whom she'd shared too much with. She realized that the Sybils out there would always be his type.

What the hell was wrong with her? Plain, boring. As far as Mark Friessen was concerned, everything about their relationship would, from this day forward, be only business.

Chapter 8

Mark took in the locksmith's sign as he pulled in front of Roland Shephard's. Knowing the man who was harassing Sybil was the island locksmith didn't leave him with a warm and fuzzy feeling.

The Jeep windows were down, and the day was getting hot, but he kept his jean jacket and sunglasses on and the dog in the back seat as he strode over to an open garage, hearing the grinding of metal. The man was tall and unshaved, wearing safety glasses, faded brown pants, and a T-shirt. He would easily blend in with a crowd.

Mark tapped on the side of the building, "Hello, are you Roland Shephard?" he called out loudly, not pulling off his glasses.

The man looked up and flicked off the machine he was cutting keys with. "Can I help you with something?" was all he said as he reached for a grimy towel and wiped his hands.

"Sure you can, if you're Roland Shephard."

The man pulled off his safety glasses and tucked them on top of his head, and Mark noted he was balding, the same as the chief. The eyes were the same too, he thought, but Roland didn't have a mustache and appeared far leaner than the chief.

"People call me Rolly," he said, a slight twang in his voice. Are you needing some keys cut? I'm kind of backed up, so it's going to be a few days."

Mark pulled back his jacket, showing his badge. "I'm here about Sybil Gillespie and her coffeehouse. You've been harassing her."

The man actually laughed as he tossed the towel down. "My brother know you're here?"

Here we go.

"Your brother, the chief?" Mark said. "What does that have to do with your harassing Sybil?"

The man smiled and shrugged, pulling his arms over his chest, and said nothing.

"I understand you broke something and have helped yourself to food and coffee without paying. That's theft. You threw a sandwich on the floor and walked out. That's general nuisance behavior. Your brother has spoken to you about this. You're scaring Sybil, and I can't have that."

Rolly only shook his head, the expression on his face one of pure amusement. The flicker in his eyes hinted at more mischief than Mark wanted to know. "I'm just having a little fun. She knows that. What I can't help but wonder is what my brother would say if he knew you were here." He reached for a cell phone.

The last thing Mark wanted was the chief shutting him down and telling him to look the other way, as had happened in another lifetime. "That doesn't matter. If you commit a crime, brother of the chief or not, you'll be held accountable. Sybil has asked you to stay away, yet you keep showing up and harassing her. What is your end game here? What is this really about? Some good old boy fun because you're related to the chief of police and think you can get away with it?"

Rolly shook his head again as he put his phone down. He didn't seem intimidated in the least. Mark knew he had texted someone, and his guess was that someone would be driving in soon in a cop car to shut this down and steer him away.

"I remember when Tolly said he was bringing you in as the detective. He mentioned you had some trouble where you were—trouble with authority. Said you were kind of a wildcard, but he'd rein you in, see your head was screwed on straight, make sure our island works the way it's supposed to."

Whatever he meant by that, Mark was glad he hadn't pulled his glasses off. He couldn't believe the chief had spoken out of turn about him.

"You know what, Mr. Shephard?" he said. "This isn't about me. And the chief, although he is my boss, cannot tell me to ignore a crime. It seems to me that you expect special treatment, as if you can do anything you want and the laws don't apply to you. But I have to tell you the law does apply to you. You're not above the law, even being the brother of the chief…"

He heard a car and took in the wide smile of Roland Shephard. He didn't have to turn around to know the chief was getting out of the sheriff's cruiser.

"'Bout time you got here," Roland said. "Did you know your boy detective was coming out?"

He turned to see the chief closing his door, not

pulling his gaze from him. Rolly strode right over to the chief, and Mark could see this wasn't going to end well.

"Mark, what are you doing here?" the chief drawled, his hands resting over his belt, over his gun, walking with purpose right toward him.

"Having a word with your brother about Sybil Gillespie. Glad you're here, Chief, because maybe you can explain to your brother what this is." Mark pulled the paper he'd written up from his pocket and held it out to Rolly, but it was the chief who ripped it from his hands and opened it.

The chief glanced for only a second at the order before lifting his gaze to Mark. "You're issuing a trespass ticket against my brother."

"Your brother has become a nuisance for Sybil Gillespie. She is terrified. After your last talk, Chief, he caused some property damage and made it clear to Sybil that he could do what he wanted. She doesn't want him in her café again, so this is for one year. He's not to set foot in the café. She doesn't want your brother showing up, trying to talk to her, anything. Roland, you scare her." He really emphasized the last part.

The chief squeezed the paper and let out a heavy sigh before tossing it to his brother, who was no longer smiling.

"You stay away from Sybil now," the chief said. "You can't go in her café anymore. You heard my detective. No more, Rolly. You leave her alone."

"You're seriously going to let this little shit walk in here and tell me, your brother, where I can and can't go?"

"Rolly, enough! You'll listen to me on this. You're

done. Stay away from the coffeehouse. It's her place, her place of business. She doesn't want you there."

Rolly whirled around and swatted his hand, sending a box of tools flying across the shop with a terrible crash. He had a temper, and Mark sensed that his anger could turn into something he wouldn't want to be on the wrong side of.

"Hey, you cool it down, there!" the chief snapped. "Get your head on straight and knock it off."

Rolly lifted both hands in the air as if to say, *Fine*. He still had his back to them, but then he looked right over at Mark with an expression he didn't much like.

"Mark, you're done here," was all the chief said.

Mark took in Roland, who was still watching him. Something made him think this wouldn't be the last he saw of him. But he started walking out of the shop, past the chief.

As he walked, the chief slapped a hand on his shoulder to stop him and leaned in, saying in a low voice, "I told you I'd take care of it. But you just had to pull your cowboy shit."

Mark only grunted, glancing back over his shoulder. "You did tell me that, but when I saw Sybil last night, I saw a girl who's terrified of your brother. Your warnings only had him harassing her more. If your brother breaks that order and walks in there, I will arrest him."

The chief pulled his hand away and gestured with his thumb to Mark's Jeep. "I'm going to be here a bit yet, Mark," he said. "Carmen is handling a complaint about some ATVs tearing up some property on the north end, so go on out there and give her a hand. And one more thing, Mark." The chief turned to him, and Roland Shephard was watching them from inside the shop. "If you ever overstep with my family again, not even Gail will be able to save your job. Then, I assure you, the closest you'll come to working in law enforcement again will be as a security guard at some mall."

Exactly what Mark had expected.

Chapter 9

"What's going on?" Mark said, taking in Carmen, who was wearing sunglasses, and the flashing lights of the big tow truck that had loaded up two of the four ATVs that had been cutting through twelve acres of property, tearing up the grass of one of the newer residents of the island.

Mark hated these nuisance calls. Seeing two of the ATV guys climbing into the pickup truck they'd left parked at the side of the road, he let out a heavy sigh. "Billy Jo isn't answering me," he said. "Left four messages on her cell phone. She was looking into something this morning that isn't sitting right with me. I'm starting to get the feeling she's ducking my calls now."

Carmen looked up at him in a way that made him feel she was laughing at him. "What did you do?" she said.

There it was, the accusation, as if this were in some way his fault.

"Nothing! Seriously. We had dinner at the chief and

Gail's last night, and she was supposed to look into something this morning and then call me back, but I haven't heard from her. Even when I called the office this last time, Pam said she was there and went to put me through, but next she was coming back on the line and saying Billy Jo couldn't take my call and would call me back. She was busy. Like, what is that?"

He knew he was frowning. He wasn't a fool, and he'd picked up on the edge in Pam's voice when she came back on the line. He knew something was going on and Billy Jo was avoiding his calls. Why?

"Sounds like you did something."

"I didn't do anything, Carmen. Besides, this is about a problem that could have me out of a job. What do you know about the chief and his family?"

Carmen pulled her sunglasses down her nose, peering over the rims with her dark eyes, then waved off the big tow truck with the impounded ATVs of the two drivers who had mouthed off. The other two had been smarter, more apologetic, and were leaving with just a fine, a dressing down, and the promise to stay off private property.

"Am I going to want to hear this?" she said.

Maybe he should have asked Carmen the night before, but then, she hadn't come back to the office by the time he'd left.

"I guarantee you not, but unfortunately, I can't unhear it, and if it's true…" He glanced off to the side, unable to finish the sentence, then dragged his gaze back to her.

She wiped her hand over her face. "I don't know the chief's family. I, unlike you, have never been invited over, and I tend to keep my nose out of what the chief and his family are doing. I learned long ago to keep my focus on myself and what's good for me. And what's good for me is keeping my nose out of my boss's business. Maybe you should do the same."

There it was, the kind of advice he didn't want.

"Can't do that if a crime has been committed," he said. "And this is the kind of crime, if the allegations are true, that could destroy the family. Hell, I don't think I want to be on the island when the shitshow comes down on them."

Carmen shoved her glasses back on and looked to the side, maybe to figure out what to say or not to say. But it was clear she was rattled. "And Billy Jo knows?"

He nodded. "She was the one who was approached the other night about a crime going on right under the nose of the chief. We just weren't sure if it was on the chief's side of the family or Gail's. Unfortunately, as we found out last night, it's Gail's."

Carmen opened her mouth to say something, then nodded, pulling her arms over her chest. "Did you talk to the chief about it…?" She let her words trail off, evidently from the expression on Mark's face.

"I'm not taking this to the chief, not this. He'd bury it after firing my ass for good this time."

Carmen nodded. "I suppose you'd better tell me."

He took in the noisy tow truck halfway down the road, its flashing lights now off, and wondered for a moment how she'd respond. "The chief can't know, not yet."

She nodded again. "Fine," was all she said in that way of hers.

"You know Cheyenne Potter? She's the niece of…"

"I know Cheyenne. She owns that little spa in town, does nails and makeup and stuff like that. She's Gail's niece. Patrice and Randy Potter are her parents. What does this have to do with her?"

"Well, this is where it gets weird and where Billy Jo comes in. When we were out for dinner the other night, she was approached in the bathroom by someone who wouldn't give her name but knew Cheyenne and the family. From the sounds of it, she knows them quite well, and she said someone in the family had been hurting Cheyenne. She was molested when she was a kid, by the sounds of it, and Billy Jo has a pretty good idea, from last night, who did it."

Carmen gasped and then stiffened. He was positive he'd never seen her at a loss for words before. The look on her face was one of shock, disbelief. "And you think someone in the chief and Gail's family did this? Are you crazy?"

Okay, so she didn't believe it. He didn't think he'd ever seen this expression from her before. She looked away and then back to him, shaking her head, before sweeping her hand in front of her face and stepping back.

"That was my first reaction, too, but I'm not so sure now," he said.

Carmen shuffled her feet and kicked a small rock to the side of the road. "There's no way. I've seen that family. Gail and her sisters, Bev and Patrice… You have to be wrong about this. Who did the woman say did it? What did Cheyenne say?"

He shrugged. "Billy Jo went to see Cheyenne this morning, booked an appointment for her nails. She was supposed to call me right after, but she didn't. As I said, I've left messages. The last time, I called the office and spoke to Pam. Maybe she struck out." He shrugged again. That was the only thing he could think of—except Billy Jo didn't give up or strike out. She came at the problem from another direction, like a wrecking ball at times.

Carmen let out a rude noise and shook her head again. "I doubt it. That girl is persistent. There has to be something else, Mark. She said she went to see Cheyenne? I hope you're wrong about it. This would kill Gail."

He lifted his hands. Maybe that was why he was stuck with that off feeling he'd had since the moment this mess with the chief's family landed on his doorstep. "Well, I would sure like to know what's going on."

Carmen looked away, thinking. "Are you sure about Cheyenne?"

He really hoped not, but after the Rolly incident that morning, he was starting to think the chief's family hid some ugly skeletons. "I wish I wasn't, but it's starting to feel that way."

Carmen nodded. "Word of advice, Mark. Gail and her sisters, Bev and Patrice, have always been really close. If this is true, take it to Gail first, not the chief."

He didn't know if he agreed, so he said nothing.

"And as far as Billy Jo," Carmen continued, "I don't know what you see in that girl, by the way, because she's like a dog with a bone. But, nevertheless, why don't you drive over there to her office and corner her? You should be good at that. Find out why she's blowing you off. Sounds to me like you did something."

He watched as Carmen strode over to her cruiser. "I

didn't do anything!" he called out, but she only waved her hand at him as she pulled her door open.

All he could think as she slid behind the wheel was what Gail had said about her. She did the same job as him, maybe more at times, and yet he made more money. Then she was driving away.

Mark stared at his Jeep and his dog, whose head was hanging out the window. He couldn't figure out why the hell Billy Jo was avoiding him.

BILLY JO'S CAR WAS IN THE PARKING LOT, AND HIS CELL phone still hadn't rung.

As Mark yanked on the handle of his Jeep, he paused for a moment, taking in the panting dog. "Last stop, I promise, and then back to the station, where you can get some water, some kibbles, and some sleep." He ran his hand over the dog's head in the passenger seat and climbed out, then closed the door.

He pulled his phone from his pocket as he walked to the front door. Of course it would be locked, so he dialed the office number.

"DCFS. This is Pam…"

"Hey, Pam, it's Mark again," he said. "Is Billy Jo there?"

There was silence for a moment. He lifted his shades and settled them on top of his red hair, then cupped his hand, looking into the window.

"No, sorry, Mark. She had an emergency and had to go out."

Her voice told him everything he needed to know. As he peered in, he could just make out Pam behind her desk in the distance, and he thought Billy Jo was also standing there, gesturing.

"Really, without her car?" he said quite directly.

"Excuse me?" Pam's voice caught.

He could come right out and bust her, but now he knew there was a problem. He hated these fucking games. "Well, see, I'm standing right outside your office, staring at her car, looking in the glass door right at you. Yup, there we go. Look at me, right here." He lifted his hand and waved, taking in the shock on her face. "And tell Billy Jo I see her."

Pam was now standing, and Billy Jo was looking right at him.

He hung up the phone and yanked on the door. "Open the door!" he yelled, then fisted his hand and pounded on it.

Billy Jo was now walking his way, and she stopped at the door without a smile, just her familiar pissed-off expression. She flicked the deadbolt and pushed open the door without trying to hide her disdain for him, which he hadn't seen in a very long time.

Okay, evidently, there was a problem.

"What is this? You're blowing me off, ignoring my calls?" he said, his hand on the door. He strode in and forced her to step back, and she let out a heavy sigh. From across the room, Pam mouthed, *Sorry*.

"I'm busy, is all," she said. A pissed-off woman. He was familiar with this.

"Hmm, games I don't have time for. What is this? Now you're avoiding my calls. What's going on with you?"

She fisted her hands at her sides, and he wondered whether she wanted to slug him. "Nothing. I just had a reality check, is all. With the Cheyenne thing, I didn't find out anything useful—aside from the fact that as soon as you dropped me off last night, you raced over to the coffeehouse girl to take up where you had left off."

Oh, shit!

"I can tell by your face that it's true. Busted, Mark. Should I say sorry? Think, now. What bothers me is this dancing around you do—but who you see really isn't my business, anyways. I mean, we're just friends, right? So let's just forget it. It shouldn't matter."

How had she found out? He could see now that the anger coming at him was really hurt. "Wait, Billy Jo. It's not what you think," he said, then reached for her arm, but she only lifted her hands and went to step back.

"Mark, it's fine. You don't owe me an explanation. I'm pretty sure you've already told me you're attracted to women you shouldn't go for. She's your type. I get it. Again, it's not my business. You can let go of me now."

He did, and she shrugged and pulled at the ratty cardigan she wore in the air-conditioned office. "It is your business, Billy Jo. I'm not sure what you heard, but I stopped to see her at the coffeehouse because she's being harassed by the chief's brother. I went as a cop, Billy Jo, not to start something up with her. Look, I should have told you."

He stepped closer to her, and she didn't step back. He could see she didn't know what to say. A silent Billy Jo was not familiar to him. He took in her frown, then ran his hand over her shoulder.

"I think we're a little more than friends," he said. He slid his hand to her chin, touching her soft skin, seeing the fire in her eyes—and panic too, he thought.

He didn't think. He just leaned in and pressed a kiss

to her lips. Soft, unexpected. He pulled back when he heard a knock at the door behind them.

Pam was still standing there, shocked, wide eyed, so Billy Jo pushed open the door to reveal a dark-haired woman, who strode in and looked from him to her.

"I'm wondering if I could talk to you," the woman said.

Billy Jo lifted her gaze to him, no longer wanting to punch him in the face. "Of course," she said. "Sure. Uh, Mark, this is Cheyenne Potter. Cheyenne, this is Detective Mark Friessen. He's a…good friend of mine."

Cheyenne only nodded, looking from Billy Jo to Mark. "You're the new detective. You work for my aunt and uncle…"

He could see she was already one step out the door.

"I can't have them knowing I'm here," she said.

"I'm a detective, Cheyenne. I'm not sharing with anyone that you're here."

Billy Jo looked over to him. "That's right, Cheyenne. Whatever you say won't leave this office. You have our word on it."

Cheyenne only nodded and made a face as if considering it. "You said some things when you came into my shop this morning. Why did you really show up and tell me that story? Because I can't shake the feeling that you didn't really want your nails done. Am I right?"

"Tell her the truth," Mark said to Billy Jo.

Cheyenne's hard gaze landed on him. "The truth?" she said sharply. "Okay, what is this?"

Billy Jo turned back to her. "The reason I showed up was because someone you know came to me about something that happened to you when you were young. Something horrible."

Cheyenne said nothing. She glanced to the door and let out a rough laugh—an odd laugh, he thought, as she shook her head. "I see," she said, then dragged her gaze over to him. "Well, even if something did happen, and I'm not saying it did, what I can tell you is that I can't talk about it. Not to you, not to anyone."

Chapter 10

What the hell had Mark been thinking, kissing her?

Billy Jo was running after Cheyenne, who'd stormed out the door, and where was Mark but still standing inside her office with Pam? The last thing she wanted to talk to him about was that kiss.

This couldn't be happening!

"Cheyenne, wait," she called out.

Cheyenne hurried with determination to a really nice red Jeep, new and shiny and expensive. She held the door open, about to climb in, when she turned back to Billy Jo, ready to give her a piece of her mind. "What do you want from me?"

"The truth is all I want. Is it true? Did someone hurt you?"

Cheyenne didn't look at her now. Billy Jo could see something so familiar in this woman.

"Look, I've been where you are," she said. "Well, maybe not exactly, but I grew up in a system where I knew no one would believe me. My mom and dad did, but even after being adopted and pulled from that, it's not something you can ever shake. When a man does that kind of thing to you… Let's just put our cards on the table and say it. What your friend said happened to you, it kills a part of you and who you were going to be."

Cheyenne was still holding the door as she looked over to her and past her to Mark, who Billy Jo realized was now standing there too. He said nothing. She knew he didn't know everything that had happened to her.

"Rhonda shouldn't have gone to you," Cheyenne said.

So it was true.

"So you know who it was who sought me out?" Billy Jo said. "She wouldn't give me her name, likely because of the chief, your uncle. She was afraid of what might come back on her. Why don't we go inside, to my office, and talk?" Billy Jo added, seeing Cheyenne was one step from climbing into her Jeep.

"Are you going to report this to Tolly and Gail?" She was looking right at Mark, and he didn't look away from her.

"No, I have nothing to tell them. You heard Billy Jo. This stays here, but let me be clear. If the chief is part of this and knows about it, I will go after him."

Billy Jo was familiar with trust issues. What she was seeing on the face of this woman was the same thing she saw every morning in the mirror. "Mark won't say anything, Cheyenne. Please, let's go in." She gestured and did her best to look over to Mark, but the way he was looking at her made her uneasy. She didn't think she could handle a supportive Mark right now.

Cheyenne closed her door. "And what about Pam?" She took a step toward her and gestured to the building.

"She has no idea what this is about. We'll go in my office. She can't hear anything," Billy Jo said, then led the way back inside, and Mark flicked the deadbolt behind them.

"Ah, Billy Jo, Grant has called a couple times…" Pam said, the phone to her ear.

Billy Jo held up her hand. "I'll talk to him later. Listen, you can head home early. I have a meeting. Just forward the calls to my voicemail."

Pam gave her an odd look. "Hi, Cheyenne. Everything okay?"

Right. Pam knew almost everyone on the island.

"Fine, Pam," Billy Jo said. "Cheyenne is just helping me with something she saw, you know, for our confidential files." She wondered at times about Pam's discretion. "She did my nails this morning, see?" She lifted her hands, hoping Pam wouldn't go flapping her mouth off. "When did you last get your nails fixed?"

"It's been some time, unfortunately," Pam said. "Okay, then, I'm going to take off. My fridge and cupboards at home are empty, and the laundry is piling up. It'll be nice to get caught up and restocked."

Billy Jo could just make out Mark saying something to Cheyenne. They were off to the side, out of the way.

Pam strode right over to Billy Jo, then flicked her gaze to Mark and back to her. She said in a low voice, "He kissed you! You two, uh…?" She gestured rather unsubtly.

"It's complicated," was all Billy Jo managed to get out.

"Mm-hmm. Isn't it always?" She walked away and lifted her hand. "See you all later."

Billy Jo tilted her head back and let out a breath as she listened to the door, hearing it lock behind Pam. She started to the hallway where the office was, where they held any closed-door meetings, and gestured to the sofa.

Cheyenne sat, and Mark closed the door. Billy Jo didn't bother turning on the lights, opting for the dimness and a little sunlight that managed to peek through the blinds. There was just something about easy lighting that made dealing with difficult issues bearable.

"As I said, I can't talk about anything even if I wanted to," Cheyenne said.

Mark was leaning against the closed door, his arms crossed, and he didn't pull his gaze from Cheyenne as he said, "You said that before, but I don't understand what that means." He had a way of talking that was so matter of fact. He never danced around anything.

"You do. It means a legal agreement," she said. "It's done all the time to prevent the truth from coming out."

Mark dragged his gaze over to Billy Jo. "A nondisclosure," he said. There he was again, the Mark she felt too comfortable sharing everything with.

Billy Jo only nodded. "Yeah, I got that. Sneaky. So when your friend came to see me, do you know what she told me?"

Cheyenne had one hand on the arm of the sofa, tapping her fingers. "You said something about believing it was okay, that it felt good. That's crazy stuff."

Billy Jo shook her head. The way Mark looked to her, she knew he didn't understand. "It's why most victims don't come forward," she said. "Because they don't think they're victims. They think they were chosen.

You know, stranger danger is such a myth, as over ninety percent of abuse happens right in children's own families. He made you feel special, didn't he? He listened to you when no one else would. He probably spent more time with you than the adults. But no one saw it, did they? Or they probably just said he was great with kids, right?"

She couldn't look at Mark, feeling the way the energy had changed in the room. Cheyenne sat so still and stared right at her.

"For a predator to do what he does," Billy Jo continued, "there has to be trust. He always chooses the child with low self-esteem, because a child who is confident would bust his ass. These guys are really good at what they do. They work their victims, making them feel good through the grooming process. They're smart, conniving, manipulative—the best liars ever. It starts with a back rub, a foot rub, listening to you with a hand on your shoulder, or cuddling on the sofa together. Then you carry this shame, but because it felt good, you convince yourself it can't be wrong. So you tell no one."

Cheynne flicked her gaze over to her. "Is that what happened to you?"

The last thing Billy Jo wanted to do was talk about herself and her fucked-up childhood. "What happened to me was different in some ways, but it killed who I was, who I was going to be. Children have a light in their eyes, and abuse kills that spirit in them, and they don't get it back. It directs them along another path. I guess that's why I do what I do, so another child doesn't have to go through what I did."

Cheyenne only nodded.

Billy Jo could feel Mark watching her, and she

wished he wouldn't. She wished he'd look away, because she didn't want to share the ugliness he was listening to. He would be disgusted with her, and then they would go back to just working together. Maybe this was a good thing.

"You know, I was looking at a family photo yesterday, a reunion," Billy Jo said. "Gail showed it to me, and there you were. Who was the man behind you with his hand on your shoulder?"

Cheyenne tapped her hand on the sofa again. "That's my uncle, Philip Maddox. He's married to my aunt Bev."

Billy Jo already knew that, but the way Cheyenne pulled in a breath and looked over to her confirmed her suspicions. "Your mom is Patrice, right?"

Cheyenne was looking right at her as she nodded. "Yes. It seems you already know that. My mom and Bev are super close, and Gail too."

Billy Jo only nodded. "You know, one of the worst parts of this is that it happens right under the noses of parents who don't see it. They have no idea which red flags to look for. These men are super smart, too. They know how to lie, how to manipulate and explain it away, their interest. It could be a caring uncle or even a father who has sole custody."

Cheyenne flicked her gaze to Billy Jo with alarm. "My dad would never do that!"

"No, but he didn't stop it, did he?"

"Do you know I told my mother? I called her crying from my aunt's house because I knew he was going to rape me. And all she did was drive over and pick me up, then bring me home. She said nothing. This was her sister, and do you know how she handled it?"

Billy Jo didn't want to look at Mark, because she could see in his face that he didn't get it.

"She didn't tell her, did she?" Billy Jo said.

Cheyenne made a face and shook her head. "I was called a liar, told to stop this. My dad said he didn't want him around me, but he didn't stop it. And you know what really sucks is that when my mom spotted him cheating on my aunt with another woman, she told Gail, who drove over and sat down with Bev. Bev said she suspected something, and she asked him to leave, but he pleaded for a second chance, and now they're getting counseling. I have a signed NDA and a nice fat bank account, but I still have to see him on holidays.

"Again, though, we're not really having this conversation. Rhonda shouldn't have gone to you, because I chose to take the money he gave me. He paid for my school, which I didn't finish, and he paid for the lease on my shop, and he bought me a new Jeep, and I now own a house. But what gets me is their outrage was about him having an affair with another woman. There was no mention of what he did to me. But then, that's something you never talk about in a family." She lifted her index finger to her mouth.

Billy Jo didn't think she'd ever seen Mark so shocked. "Unfortunately, an affair is the easier evil to deal with. The other is so bad that it's easier to say it can't be true." Billy Jo knew she sounded too calm. "When did you sign this NDA, this legal agreement? Who knew about it?"

"Right after I broke off my engagement. I showed up at his house in the middle of the night, crying because of what he did to me. A lawyer was contacted, his, and I took the money because I was owed it. At least this way I wouldn't have to work so hard. But Rhonda was furious—which is likely why I'm here now. I need to tell you to stop, please. Stop looking into this. Stop everything, because as he said to me, I was complicit. I was part of it. It wasn't all on him. And you know what? He was right," Cheyenne said. She reached for her bag.

Billy Jo linked her fingers together in front of her, looking up at Mark, who didn't have to say how he was feeling, as it was written all over him.

"Did the chief and Gail know?" he said.

Cheyenne was now standing and lifted her hands in a helpless gesture. "I don't know. Maybe, or maybe they were just like everyone else and chose not to see, not wanting to know."

"So that's it? You're just going to walk out the door?" Mark said. "Let me bring him in, arrest him, charge him…"

But she was already shaking her head. "You can't. As I said, I can't testify. He made sure of it. And I wouldn't, anyway. You think I want people to know?" She was so matter of fact. She took a step and then looked down at Billy Jo. "I'm sorry for what you went through, but I don't think it was the same." Then she motioned for Mark to move away from the door, which he did, and she pulled it open. When she glanced back, she said, "If he did it to me, am I the only one? Or could he have done it to someone else in the family?"

Then she was gone, out the door.

Mark gestured to Billy Jo, but she just lifted her hand and said, "Let her go. But she's right, Mark, and that's likely why she came. This man is thriving in the Shephard family, and a man like that doesn't stop with just one."

Mark pulled his hand over his face. "You think that's

why she showed up here? I've never had to deal with this. I'm feeling a little out of my depth."

She could see that. "She knows something, Mark," she said, sitting in the padded office chair. When he lowered his gaze to her, what she saw looking back was something she didn't want.

"We've never talked about what happened to you," he said. "Maybe we should."

She glanced down at her hands. "Mark, you think I want to have you looking at me as if I'm damaged?" She lifted her gaze to him.

He frowned. "That's not how I see you," he said. But maybe he realized how uncomfortable she was, as he only shook his head and said, "I think it's time to have a talk with Gail."

"You know you can't tell her about Cheyenne coming here and what she said. You promised her."

"And I'll keep my word, but it's time to find out what Gail knows, what the chief knows. Because if there is someone else, I plan to put this guy away." He let his gaze linger on her as he glanced out into the hall. "You coming?"

"Why not? At least this way I can make sure you don't say anything about Cheyenne."

He let her walk past him, offering her that arrogant smile that did a number on her, and then ran his hand over her back when she stepped past him.

Oh, boy. She was really in trouble with Mark.

Chapter 11

"Just so you know, full disclosure, I'm kind of in the hot seat with the chief," Mark said.

Billy Jo was wearing sunglasses, and he couldn't tell what she was thinking from where she sat in the passenger side as he drove not to the station but to the Shephards' house. The dog had already made it clear from the way he licked Billy Jo's face how much he missed her.

"Is this something new or the same old?" she said.

Mark took in Gail's parked white Tacoma, grateful that the chief wasn't there, as he pulled in and parked. Then he took a second to really look at Billy Jo. He hadn't understood what she'd been through. Hearing what she'd said to Cheyenne, he wondered how much of that was true for her.

"You know how I mentioned his brother, Roland Shephard, was harassing Sybil? Well, I slapped him this morning with a trespass ticket barring him from entering her café for a year." Mark turned off his Jeep.

Billy Jo seemed to be taking in what he'd said. She

was so damn hard to read sometimes. He still couldn't believe he'd kissed her.

"The chief showed up when I was there," he continued, "and he was furious with me, but I wouldn't back down. So, to be clear, it seems I really am stepping into his family, and there's going to be a breaking point."

Billy Jo said nothing as she stepped out of the Jeep, and the dog whined because he knew where he was. Mark let him out and closed the door before walking around to where Billy Jo was waiting. He stopped, seeing how closed off she was, and rested his arm on the front of the Jeep, then lifted his sunglasses and settled them in his red hair.

"To be clear, I won't lie to you, and I'm not looking to date anyone else," he said. "I can see how uncomfortable you are talking about it."

"You're the one talking, not me," she cut in with pure snark, and he couldn't help the smile that tugged at his lips.

He heard the door pull open, likely because the dog had been scratching.

"What are you two doing here?" said Gail. "Hey, Lucky, I'm all out of bones." She rubbed the dog, and he trotted into the house.

Mark walked over to the door, Billy Jo right beside him.

"We wanted to talk to you, Gail, if you have a minute," Billy Jo said before he could say anything. He glanced down to her as she pulled off her sunglasses and rested them on top of her head.

"Yeah, of course. Come on in. Can I get you two something to drink? Mark, you're still on call, so no beer."

He only lifted his hand. "Nothing for me, Gail."

He wiped his cowboy boots and watched as Billy Jo slipped off her flats and walked barefoot into the kitchen, following Gail. The house was big, a family home, and it was always so neat and tidy. He really didn't know how to start, and he hoped Gail didn't know what the man her sister was still married to had done.

He heard Billy Jo ask for a glass of water, and Gail was just filling it, along with a bowl of water for the dog, when he strode in.

"I really hate doing this, Gail," Mark said, "but I need to talk to you about someone in your family who has done something pretty bad…"

"Tolly already told me about what happened with his brother," she said. "Rolly and Tolly. I think his mom had an odd sense of humor, naming them virtually the same thing, but Rolly has always been a handful. Don't worry, Mark. He'll honor that trespass and leave her alone, and if he doesn't, then you go and pick him up. Tolly can't keep cleaning up after his brother. How is Sybil doing, anyway? Maybe I should stop in and see her to let her know we're serious about keeping him away."

Mark shook his head. "Sybil is scared he's going to hurt her. You should know the only thing the chief's talk with him accomplished was to have him right back in her café, causing more damage, making his point that he can do anything he wants. She's worried he'll be waiting for her, and maybe next time he'll hurt her."

Gail firmed her lips, and Billy Jo watched him closely.

"No woman or even young girl should ever have to worry about a man and what he could do to her," he said, not looking away from Billy Jo as he said it, hoping Gail couldn't see how uncomfortable she was. "Which is why we're here, Gail."

Billy Jo couldn't look at him anymore. She leaned on the island and hadn't touched the glass of water.

Gail dragged her gaze between the two of them. "Why do I have the feeling we're not talking about Rolly? Okay, you two, spill, whatever it is." Gail rested both her hands on the counter.

"You're right," he said. "We're here about someone on your side of the family. You have someone in your family who pays more attention to the children than the adults?"

By the way she dragged her gaze between the two of them, he wasn't sure whether she was going to laugh. "Are you serious? What the hell is this?"

He gestured toward her. "Someone came forward about Philip Maddox, your sister's husband. He may have been inappropriate…"

"Cut the crap, you two. You're talking about my sister's husband. Whoever told you that is wrong," she said. "But he is a cheat. I told Bev to cut him loose, but she wouldn't listen. She let him talk her into therapy. Is he cheating on Bev again? Is that what this is?"

Mark had never felt this uncomfortable. If he hadn't known before, he did now. Gail had no idea. How could she not have seen?

"He's molesting young girls. We don't know how many," Billy Jo said, and he couldn't get over how calm she sounded.

Her mouth fell open. "You're serious!"

Billy Jo only nodded.

"Gail," Mark said, "the problem is that we know one

girl he's done it to, but she signed a nondisclosure agreement in exchange for cash, so she can't talk about it. But there's more. You see him paying extra attention to the kids, the girls?"

She said nothing for a second, then let out a rough sigh. "He's always liked kids, always been the one who knew how to talk to them when no one else did. He and Bev have three kids, two girls and a boy. Who is it that this happened to? Not someone in our family."

Mark shook his head. "Can't tell you that. Gave my word."

Gail leaned back, her eyes widening. "Did Cheyenne tell you this?" The way she spat it out sounded so accusing.

"Gail, this isn't about Cheyenne," Billy Jo cut in.

"Oh, yes it is. Philip told us he paid for Cheyenne's school and wanted to help her out, and he said not to tell Patrice. I didn't agree, but Bev said she'd been having a hard time. Sure enough, she didn't even finish school. She dropped out and came back here to hit him up for more money. He helped her start that salon. He helped her… No matter what kind of dirty dog he is, cheating on my sister, he gave more to Cheyenne than…" Then Gail stopped talking.

"Gail, it sounds to me as if Philip has really managed to destroy Cheyenne's credibility so no one will believe her," Billy Jo said. "I have a hard time believing an uncle who isn't even related by blood would do all that for his niece. I know well the lies predators tell. The thing they're really, really good at is destroying credibility so their victims won't be believed. Who else is he doing that to, giving extra attention? Come on, think about it. I can tell you that parents, adults, miss those red flags all the time. How often do you see the girls sitting on his lap, or he's cuddling them, down on the floor, playing with them? When all you adults are together, where is he?"

"Stop!" Gail held up the flat of her hand to Billy Jo, who he knew was getting through to her, and then put her fingers on her forehead, pressing into it. "Oh my God, no, no, no…"

He'd never seen Gail this upset.

She blew out a breath and flicked her gaze over to him. "I'm going to talk to my sister," she said. Then she shut her eyes for another second as if having trouble understanding what she was hearing. "You need to go, Mark. Not a word of this to Tolly. Do you hear me?"

Something about Gail now left him with an off feeling.

"What are you going to do, Gail?" he said, then glanced over to Billy Jo, seeing the alarm in her expression.

"You said you think he's gone after a girl in my family. If he is the monster you're saying he is…" She only shook her hand and gestured rather sharply. "Go back to work, Mark, now."

Billy Jo slid her hand over his arm and said, "Mark, let's go," then patted her leg so Lucky would follow her to the front door. That left just Mark and Gail.

"Don't do anything stupid, Gail," he said.

"You need to mind your own business, Mark."

He only nodded. Gail didn't pull her gaze from him: hard, angry, and unforgiving. Definitely not someone he wanted to be on the wrong side of. So he started to the front door, which Billy Jo was already walking through, and over to the Jeep, where she had pulled the door open and let the dog in, then slid inside.

As Mark climbed behind the wheel, he took in Gail, who was now walking out the front door as well, keys in hand and her bag too, right over to her pickup.

"Should I be worried?" he said, then dragged his gaze to Billy Jo.

"I don't know, Mark. But whatever happens now, at least Gail has her eyes wide open."

Chapter 12

"I'm not sleeping with you, Mark," Billy Jo said.

She didn't miss the twitch of his lips in reply. He had the lid of an old propane barbecue open and fired up on his deck, and she hadn't realized she was so hungry as she listened to the sizzle and breathed in the aroma of the two burgers he'd insisted on cooking.

"Look, I'm just feeding you. Don't read something more into it." He flipped a burger over on the grill, and the flames flickered. The dog was curled up on the deck at her feet, asleep, and she held a glass of red wine that Mark had poured for her and handed her without even asking. That was the worst thing, that he knew exactly what she liked.

"You sure this isn't about Sybil? You know, Mark, one of the things I'm very aware of is how much I'm not your type. Remaining friends is probably a better idea…"

He turned and squinted in the sun, which was falling in the sky, facing her with a look that could have turned water to ice. "Billy Jo, this is really beginning to piss me off. Maybe I should have told you about Sybil, going to see her because she was in trouble, but I don't tell you every case I'm working on, and I'm pretty sure you don't share your cases. Anyway, it was Sybil, so it's my mistake, but that doesn't mean you get to toss out what you think my type is, just because I've always gone for the ones that—"

"Mark, you have a tattoo on your arm of your former girlfriend as a reminder that love is for fools. Wasn't that what you told me? You like to mess around. And I've picked up on the fact that you've clearly had your heart broken one too many times. I get it, but to be clear, I don't mess around."

This was getting so damn uncomfortable, all because she couldn't shake that kiss or the fact that she was pretty sure it had been meant to convince himself more than her that she was right for him. But they were still dancing around the issue, and she was more sure than ever that he could and would break her.

"Look, I don't have a great history with women," he said. "I have great parents, so there's no excuse. But I think this is more about you." He gestured with the spatula.

For a moment, she thought he'd lost his mind. "Me? Now you're turning this on me? What the hell does your relationship history have to do with me?"

He lifted his beer and tilted it to her, making a rude sound under his breath, before he took a swallow. "You know, you went through some pretty bad shit, and maybe I don't have any idea what to do about it, what to do for you, or how I can make it better. We hang out, we go out for dinner, I go over to your place, and you're sitting here now at mine. It's what we do. We're friends, sure, but I always drop you off after.

"And you know I care. I listened to what you said to Cheyenne, and even before that, I knew a little about what you've been through. But I need you to tell me your comfort level, your boundaries, and maybe how the hell you're feeling, because I'm out in uncharted territory. You were abused, badly, yet you've survived. I very clearly heard you say today that that kind of abuse kills who you are, who you were going to be, and your soul.

"Can I fix it? I don't know how. You have to help me out here, Billy Jo, and maybe tell me what happened. Who hurt you, when, how? I look at you now, and I see how much you hold on to everything. I see your freaked-out expression, like now." He gestured to her again, holding his beer to her. "But you have to let me in."

She lifted her glass of wine, her heart hammering, and took a swallow. Then Mark's phone started ringing, a welcome interruption.

"Great," was all he said as he put his beer down and reached for his phone on the old table outside. "Hello? Yeah… No, no, what the fuck? No, I'll be right there." He had his back to her now. "Yes, I said I'm on my way." Then he hung up, walked over to the barbecue, and flicked it off.

She leaned forward, seeing how he'd suddenly gone into cop mode. "What's going on?"

He kept walking into the house, and the dog even stood up and wandered inside after him. "That was Carmen. There's been a shooting," he called out from inside.

She was on her feet, seeing he was two minutes from driving away, which would leave her stuck at his place without a car. She walked inside and put her wine on the counter. Mark had his gun holstered, his jean jacket back on, and his keys in hand.

"Do you know who's been shot and what happened?" She reached for her bag on the sofa and slung it over her shoulder.

He shook his head. "Philip Maddox…"

She could feel herself leaning in from the shock.

Mark gestured to her face. "Yeah, my thoughts exactly." He was at the door, and the dog had already strode outside again. "Lucky, get back in here. You're staying with Billy Jo."

She was shaking her head. "I'm coming too, Mark. Don't even think of telling me no. He was shot?"

Billy Jo was out the door now, too, though the dog trotted back inside. Mark pulled the door closed behind him and pulled the lid down on the barbecue, the burgers still on, as he strode past. Long legs, long stride.

"I don't know," he said. "Carmen just said there's been a shooting at his property and she's on her way out there. That's all I know."

Mark moved fast when he was in a hurry, and he was already at his Jeep and inside by the time she hurried around to the passenger side and climbed in. She'd just reached for her seatbelt when he had the jeep in gear and backed up, swinging around, driving down a driveway flanked by overgrown bushes on each side, out to the road.

There was something about his hard, chiseled face. His gaze was laser focused, and she knew that the conversation she hadn't wanted to have was now forgotten.

WEST COAST LUXURY WAS ALL SHE COULD THINK OF AS Mark drove up to a property with the most breathtaking views, through a double iron gate that opened electronically. She could see both the chief and Carmen were there, and the scene didn't look good.

Mark pulled in and parked behind Carmen's cruiser, then turned off the Jeep and was out the door without a word to her. She took her time climbing out and stepping onto the driveway.

The chief was looking down at something, and she heard a woman crying. Carmen and Mark were now talking, as well, and Gail was also there, standing off to the side with the crying woman. Billy Jo kept walking, taking in the noise, the scene, and seeing what she thought had to be a body covered in a green tarp, blood pooling out from under it.

She took in the chief seeing it was the body he was standing over. As she strode closer, the chief looked over at her and then at Gail, who was hugging the hysterical woman.

"Why? I don't understand why!" the woman said.

Gail said something to her that Billy Jo couldn't make out. She wondered for a moment whether Mark would tell her to go sit back in the Jeep. She stopped beside him and Carmen, and both stopped talking and looked down at her.

"Is that Philip?" She gestured over to the tarp and the body.

Carmen nodded. "Dead. He took two in the chest. Was already dead when I got here."

Mark was shaking his head. "What a fucked-up mess

this is," he said under his breath before walking over to Gail, who still had her arm around the woman, who had to be her sister.

"Do you know who shot him? What happened here?" Billy Jo said.

She wasn't sure Carmen was going to answer, from the way she looked over to the chief and then Gail. She shook her head. "Not sure yet."

As Billy Jo took in the body lying there, the woman crying, and this expensive piece of property, so much of this puzzle was falling into place. There was money here, and she realized Philip Maddox evidently had the financial means to pay off Cheyenne.

Mark had pulled Gail aside and was talking to her, and something about the way they stood together, off to the side, told her to stay back and stay out of it. Gail handed a gun to Mark, who opened an evidence bag and tucked it in. Had she done it, or had she just taken the gun?

"Carmen, did Gail shoot him?" Billy Jo said.

Carmen was watching Gail and Mark, and she let out a rough sigh.

Then the chief gestured to her and barked, "Carmen, come over here."

Carmen glanced once to Billy Jo and said in a low voice, "I really hate getting involved in family stuff." Then she walked away, over to the chief, and as Billy Jo took in the crying woman, who was now standing alone, one question kept going through her mind.

Had she and Mark been the catalyst to a man lying dead in his driveway?

Chapter 13

He'd run his hand over his face a dozen times.

"Take the gun, Mark," Gail said. "You know you have to process it and work the scene. You're going to have to make sure all the Is are dotted and Ts are crossed. Tolly can't have his hand in any part of this investigation. You know that already. It has to be you. There are no rounds left. I already emptied the chamber."

Mark pulled out an evidence bag from his inside pocket and held it open as Gail reached into the pockets of her light blue jean jacket. From one she pulled the bullets, from the other the gun. Mark took the .45, a cop's gun, checked that it had no rounds, and tucked it in the bag.

"Did you shoot him, Gail? Is that why you came here, because of what Billy Jo and I told you this morning?"

She lifted her gaze to him with the kind of look that made him wish she wouldn't answer. Then she said, "I shot him."

This couldn't be happening.

"I'm going to have to read you your rights, Gail."

She nodded. "I know my rights, Mark, so consider them read—and I'm waiving them."

He shook his head and pulled the Miranda card from his pocket even though it was burned into his memory. "As you said, Gail, by the book. We're not cutting any corners here."

This was a case he knew could come back on him and burn him in ways he couldn't even imagine. So he read off the card, the Miranda rights, and took in the way she pulled in a breath, frustrated, on edge.

The chief and Carmen were walking his way.

"I told you, Mark, I understand my rights," Gail said. "You have the gun. I told you I shot him."

"I advise you very strongly not to talk to me without a lawyer," Mark said. "You know this."

"Gail, you're done here," the chief cut in.

Mark dragged his gaze over to him, wishing he'd step in and get Gail to listen, get his wife a damn lawyer. "You're going to have to take a back seat on this one, Chief," he said. "This is your family, your wife. This entire scene is something you can't have any input on. This is the kind of thing you can't investigate, because your wife shot him. Stand down."

He expected an argument. He was ready to argue.

"Tolly, Mark is right." Why did Gail sound so calm?

"Chief, the coroner is here," Carmen said, nodding in that direction.

Mark heard the whir of the electric gates, and he took in the blue sedan driving in, the old doc who was called to a crime scene when a body was found. He issued the death certificate and ruled the cause of death, and for this homicide, those details would seal Gail's fate.

He shook his head. The chief was already walking with Carmen over to the coroner and the body on the ground, but he needed to get the chief out of there, away from the crime scene.

"Jesus, Gail, what the hell did you do?" he finally said. "Is this because of me and Billy Jo coming over? You, what, took matters into your own hands? You shot him? This can't be happening. Actually, I beg you, please don't say anything else to me."

He didn't know how to be calm right now. He wanted answers from her, but at the same time, he wanted her to shut her damn mouth, because he couldn't protect her if she didn't.

"He sexually molested my niece right under my nose," she said. "I didn't know. I never saw it. How could I not see it?"

"Gail, I'm not kidding. You know the DA is going to use everything you say to me against you. It will be twisted out of context to destroy you and get a conviction…"

She reached over and touched his arm. "I left my house at roughly four fifteen this afternoon, after you and Billy Jo showed up and told me my sister's husband was a monster who had molested my niece and that there could be another victim. I showed up here and told my sister what he had done. He, of course, denied it, as he was right there in the kitchen with her. He told me I was out of my mind.

"Then I asked Bev, 'Did you ever catch him with one of the girls, doing something that didn't seem right? How many times did he explain it away, and you swallowed it?' I asked her to recall how he'd lied to her face every time he cheated on her. I asked him how many girls he'd touched, went after, targeted. Did he groom them? Did he think it was okay, as a grown man, to do what he did to them, right under our noses? While we were downstairs, laughing, was he upstairs with one of the kids, Cheyenne, doing God knows what to her?"

She was standing before him with incredible calmness, recounting details without emotion, so matter of fact. He could still hear the other woman crying and turned to see that Billy Jo was talking to her. That had to be Bev. He needed to pull her aside, too.

"He kept denying it," Gail said. "But my sister was staring at him, and she said it so bluntly, as if she saw the truth. 'You're lying,' she said to him, as if she could tell. You know, Mark, when you're married to someone as long as they were married, as long as I've been to Tolly, you know when that person is lying. Sometimes you choose not to see it, especially when they're so good at it. But when you figure it out, you realize they've been lying to you right from the beginning…"

She stopped talking, her arms crossed in front of her, and glanced over her shoulder to her sister, who was still standing with Billy Jo. "Bev asked him about Tammy. She's their youngest. He denied it, but even I could see it, and I felt this sick feeling. His own daughter… She's twelve. I could see he was lying again and again, and he would lie his way out of it. The only way to stop him was to get him to confess, because putting Tammy through that ordeal—criminal charges, a trial, being ripped apart, having to testify against her father—was not something we could do.

"So I called him out. I pulled my gun on him, and I

made him walk out of the house, onto the driveway, and get down on his knees. I told him he had one chance to tell the truth, to confess. He laughed at me and said I'd never prove it. Tammy would never talk. And he said Cheyenne couldn't talk at all. Then he lunged for the gun, and it just went off. I called Tolly first, then Carmen, and I told her to call you. You're going to need to write all this up in a report, Mark. I'll sign it."

He didn't know what to say. He wished she hadn't said anything. "You're saying it was an accident, like self defense?"

"I'm saying the gun went off when he lunged for it. Now you're going to have to book me. I'll have my lawyer meet us down there. Do up your report, Mark, and call the DA." She held out her hands to him.

He just stared. "I'm not going to cuff you, Gail. Put your hands down." He gestured toward Carmen and called out, "Carmen, take Gail back to the station."

Carmen stared at him with wide eyes. The chief was standing with the coroner, who had the tarp pulled back. Mark couldn't shake the feeling that he'd been given a story.

Gail was walking over to Carmen's cruiser and climbing into the front passenger side, and Mark walked over to the deputy, who looked at him as if he'd lost his mind.

"Seriously, Mark, what the hell am I supposed to do?" she said. "This is Gail, the chief's wife. Gail, remember?"

He pulled his hand over the back of his neck and then lowered it, feeling the tightness, the tension that pulled. "Just take her back and park her somewhere until I get there. And take this. Get it off to forensics."

He handed her the evidence bag with the gun. "Do me a favor, too. I want her tested for powder burns on her hands, and I want the prints on the gun."

Gail was sitting in the passenger side, waiting, and he knew Carmen was having as hard a time with this as he was.

"And what, exactly, do you expect to find?" Carmen said. "I heard her confess that she shot him."

He kept his voice low, looking around at this expensive house, this big property, the camera at the front door. "Don't know, but something about this just isn't sitting right with me."

Carmen made a rude noise and lifted her hand as if this was too much. He stepped back, and she walked to her cruiser, pulled open the door, slid behind the wheel, and pulled away.

Mark looked over to the chief, who was with the coroner, and Billy Jo, who was still standing with the crying wife of the man who was now dead in the driveway. He dug into each step, striding right over to the body and the chief, who nodded to the coroner and said something Mark couldn't make out.

The chief stepped back. "This one is yours, Mark. Don't screw it up," he said. Then he started walking, and he tossed out over his shoulder to the coroner, "Give my best to Wendy."

"Will do, Chief," the coroner said. The man wore glasses and had thinning hair on top, squatting down with the tarp pulled back. He squinted up at Mark, and Mark looked down at a man who, to him, was a monster.

"Can you tell me what happened here?" he said,

turning to watch the chief as he walked over to Bev and Billy Jo and said something to her.

"Shot two times, fatal…"

Mark looked into the sightless eyes of the light-haired man, tall, with a blood-soaked dress shirt that could have been white. Even he knew the bullet wounds were kill shots. Someone knew how to shoot.

"Can you tell where he was, at close range, if he was reaching for the gun when it went off?" Mark said. He felt the man's hesitation and wondered for a moment how deep his friendship went with the chief.

"I need to get him back and do an autopsy to see the trajectory, but I'm pretty sure he wasn't shot at close range. I'll pull the slugs from him and send them to the lab. I take it everything goes to you?" The coroner stood up and pulled off his rubber gloves.

"Yes, everything comes to me. And from this moment on, you do not talk to the chief."

The coroner only inclined his head. He was looking over to the chief. "Understood. But I should tell you something else," he said in a way that had Mark's stomach knotting.

"And that is?" Mark said.

The coroner looked down at the body, which was still uncovered. "I may not be the best coroner out there, as I'm an old doc first, but one thing I do know is that he wasn't shot here."

Chapter 14

An ambulance had arrived, and Billy Jo stood with her arms pulled across her chest, watching as the body, now in a body bag, was loaded onto a stretcher. The coroner was walking to his blue sedan, and the chief was still standing there with Bev, who had finally stopped crying.

"Bev, you can't stay here," he said. "Come on, I'll take you to our house. This is a crime scene…"

"And what about my sister?" Bev said. "And the girls? How am I going to tell them? This is a nightmare…"

Billy Jo didn't add anything, just watched Mark, tracking him as he talked first with the coroner, then with the paramedics who'd just loaded the body into the ambulance. Now he walked into the house.

Whatever he was doing, he was focused. That was something she had noticed about him: He never did anything halfway. He was all in, not cutting corners, the kind of man whose word, she realized, really did mean something.

"Gail will be fine. Don't you worry," the chief said. "Patrice already went to pick up the girls, too. The family has this, and your brother is on his way, as well. I've already talked to him…"

Bev only nodded.

All that kept going through Billy Jo's mind was what she'd cried out: *Why did he have to do it? He shouldn't have done it! Why, why, why…?*

The one thing she couldn't make herself say to this mother was that it was okay. Because it wasn't.

"You know, Chief, I'm pretty sure Mark will need to talk to Bev, so I don't think you should be leaving," Billy Jo said. In fact, she didn't know why Mark wasn't out there now. What the hell was he doing in the house?

The chief just gestured quite sharply and rudely for her to step aside and away from Bev, who wore a pair of white slacks and a pink shirt, not a spot of blood on her. Billy Jo wondered if she was the only one who had noticed that.

She took in the chief's expression, which said he wasn't impressed with her, as she followed him away from Gail's sister, whose eyes were still red and puffy. She resembled Gail in some ways, the face, the height.

"What do you think you're doing there, missy?" the chief snapped. "Giving your opinion on a crime scene? You have zero authority here. Why are you here, anyway?"

What was it with the way he talked down to her? Her mouth was tight, her hands crossed in fists against her sweater.

"I'm here because I was with Mark when he was called over. To be clear, I'm just pointing out that you're overstepping, Chief. I may not be a detective, but I do know that Mark needs to talk to everyone, and if you take Bev before he's talked to her, it could come back on Gail. Now, I like Gail, so I'll tell you that my dad, who's one of the best lawyers out there, taught me enough about how the law works that I know your just being here still is a problem. There will be a big spotlight shining down on this scene, and you know what the headlines will be if the chief of police is discovered working the crime scene where his wife is a prime suspect. This could be construed as tampering with evidence."

She could see from the way he stared down at her that she was only digging herself deeper into his bad side, on which she'd always been. She knew he wasn't happy with her, not in the least. In fact, she was pretty sure by how stiffly he stood that he would start in on her, or maybe he'd just put Bev in his car and drive away.

"Now listen here, girl. Let's talk about who shouldn't be here."

"Chief!" Mark snapped sharply, striding from the house. He really could move when he wanted to. "I need you to wait over by your car." He gestured with his thumb, an edge to him now that showed he wasn't messing around. Then he flicked his blue eyes to Billy Jo as he closed the distance.

She'd never seen this kind of determination in his face before. Not like this.

The chief stepped back, and Mark watched him, then stepped right in front of Billy Jo so she had to look up at him.

"What was that about?" he said.

What was she supposed to say, that she suspected the chief was trying to clean something up?

"Well, I pointed out to him that you likely need to interview Bev, because he was planning on putting her in his car and driving out of here before you had a chance to talk to her."

He lifted his gaze, about to say something. He looked back down at her and let out a heavy sigh. "Thanks," he said. "Yes, I do need to talk to her, and then the chief has to go." He pulled his hand over his face, and she could see how this was weighing on him. He was looking past her and over her head—at what, she wasn't sure. Then he shook his head, and she knew he was stuck in some dark, heavy thoughts.

"How's it looking?"

He shook his head. "Not good for Gail." He turned back to the house, gesturing to the front door, and she could see the weight of all this was solely on his shoulders. "See the camera?"

There was that knot in her stomach as she stared at a camera she hadn't seen. "Is that why you were in the house?"

He pulled his hand over his face again. "Yeah, only I can't find the footage. It has to be here somewhere, but I have this feeling I can't shake…"

He was looking off into the distance. Just being there with him, seeing who he really was, she knew there was no hope for her. God damn, she was sunk. He'd managed to find a way into her heart. She wanted to reach out and touch him, but she couldn't do that. She wouldn't. So she kept her hands fisted, tucked where they were.

"What is it?" she said.

He glanced back to the chief, who was standing by his car. Evidently, he was listening to Mark, which was good. But Billy Jo still had a few things she wanted to say, like that she didn't trust him, and that she actually had a name. Bev had wandered over and was talking with the chief again, both out of earshot.

"I feel like this entire scene was a setup," Mark said. "It's just too organized, too clean, too…something that isn't sitting right. And the coroner said something else. Maddox wasn't shot here. There's another thing, too. Do you notice anything missing?"

She wasn't sure what she was supposed to be looking at, still stuck on the revelation that the man hadn't been shot there. She found herself automatically looking over to the spot on the driveway where the body had been. The gate was swinging closed, as the ambulance and coroner were both now gone. Mark was shaking his head again, looking down at her, and she couldn't get her tongue to move.

"Gail's truck," she said. "Where the hell is her truck?" She looked around. "Holy shit, Mark, what the hell is going on here?"

Mark slid a hand over her shoulder. "You may want to wait in the Jeep. I need to have a word with the chief, with Bev. I'll piece this together. But you know who else I want to talk to?"

She only shook her head, which was still spinning, because they'd gone from trying to find a way to stop and expose this man to seeing him lying dead on the pavement. She didn't think she'd ever forget the look in Gail's eyes when she'd figured out why they'd stopped by and what her sister's husband had done.

"I would think a whole lot of people," she said, and

she thought her voice squeaked, or maybe it was the disbelief still swimming in her head.

Mark turned and looked at the house again, then back to her, thinking as if trying to put a puzzle together in his head. "Sure," he said, "but I think I'll start with all of Gail's family."

Chapter 15

When Mark stepped inside the station, what hit him first was Gail's empty desk. He dragged his gaze over to Carmen, who was sitting at her desk, her eyes on him as if waiting for someone to tell her what to do.

"Where is Gail?" he said.

She only pointed to the door that led back to the cells. Mark took in the chief's empty office, then nodded as he closed the station door behind him. He tossed his keys and sunglasses on his desk, feeling Carmen tracking his every move. When he heard the squeak of the chair and glanced over, she was looking at the closed front door.

"Where's your girlfriend?" she said.

Right now, he didn't really want to address how everyone had been tossing out that title for so long, assuming he and Billy Jo were an item when, in fact, they were stumbling around. "I dropped her off at home so she has her car. She'll check in on Lucky and take him back to her place. You put Gail in a cell?"

"No. She walked back and put herself there. What the hell am I supposed to do, Mark? I expected a lawyer or someone to walk in here. Am I charging her? What are you going to tell the DA? Then there's the chief."

Mark dragged his gaze to Carmen's desk, which was neat and tidy. "So who arrived first at the crime scene, you or the chief?"

There was something about Carmen. Her face never showed much emotion, and she was really hard to read. She lowered her gaze to the desk and tapped her fingers on it as she said, "I did."

He wondered why there was nothing on her desk, no notes, no paper, no laptop open. "And when did the chief show up, exactly? How long before me did the chief arrive?"

"Not long before you. Sounds like you're questioning me, Mark."

He leaned against his desk and crossed his arms over his chest, then pulled in a sharp breath. "You do up a report yet? You were first on the scene. What did you see when you drove in? Where was Gail? Where was Bev? Was anyone else there? And what happened to Gail's truck?"

There it was, a flicker of something. He wasn't sure he'd actually seen it.

Carmen pulled in a breath and shrugged. "Look, I'm doing what you told me to do. You're running this, remember? I brought Gail back. When I got there, the body was already covered with a tarp. Gail told me to make sure you handled the case. And I never saw her truck. I'm not sure what you're alluding to…"

"Where's the video from the camera?"

She stared long and hard, unblinking, not pulling her gaze.

"I know there's a camera at the front door," he said. "And that story Gail told about how she shot him when he lunged for the gun? I don't buy any of it. The coroner already told me Maddox wasn't shot there. The body was moved. So again, Carmen, I'm going to ask you where Gail's truck is and what happened to the video footage. You see, I talked to Bev, and what bothers me is that she confirmed Gail's story, word for word. The details didn't vary at all. But how the story matched was too neat and tidy. Then there's you."

She sat up straight, not a woman to ever cower.

"You want Gail to go down for this?" he said.

"It wasn't my idea," she replied in a low voice.

Relief and anger had him dragging his gaze to the door to the cells, then back to Carmen, who was still sitting in her chair, her hand flat on her empty and clean desk, her feet planted as if she were about to stand up.

He dragged his hand over his face. "Who is she protecting?"

Carmen rolled her shoulders as she stood, her hands on her duty belt. She flicked those dark eyes up to him. "She's Gail, Mark," she said. "She was the first person to make sure I had a place to go, to make sure the chief stays in line, to make sure you've stayed to make this island better. She knew that if the chief were left to run everything, a lot more would slip under the radar."

He took a step toward her. "I know this is Gail, but I am not covering up a crime, and right now, all I'm seeing is police coverups and corruption. This will only make it worse for Gail, for this island, for you…"

"Knock it off, you two."

He turned and took in Gail standing in the doorway, looking over to him and Carmen. From the expression on her face, she'd heard everything.

"Gail, I'm sorry, but I told you this wouldn't work," Carmen said.

Mark couldn't believe this. He found himself staring down at a woman he knew was a damn good cop. But what had she done?

"Gail, where is the video?" he said. "Who took it? There should be a laptop in the office, but I couldn't find anything. You hide it?"

Gail was such a confident woman, and he realized she was prepared to take the fall for this. She said nothing at first, instead looking at him with determination he'd never seen before, not like this. Apparently, family was everything to her.

"You should book me, Mark. I already made a statement," she said, then flicked her gaze around him to Carmen.

"No, no, no. This is not how this works," he snapped, feeling the burn of his temper rising. "So now you're putting Carmen in the crosshairs? You're telling me the chief arrived after Carmen? Where is your truck, Gail? Because what you evidently don't know is that the coroner already told me that Philip was not shot there, so that blows your story about him down on his knees on that driveway right out the window. Who moved him, Gail?"

She looked down as if considering something, a damn stubborn woman.

"You know, from the minute I drove in there, I knew something was off," he said. "And you know what's worse, Gail? Whoever you're protecting, it's going to be worse for them. The coroner is not going to lie. I will order an independent second autopsy if I have to, off this island, to get to the bottom of this and the right story, the truth."

Maybe she hadn't expected that, as she lifted her gaze to him, laced with fury.

"You know I won't cover up a crime, not for anyone," he said, taking a step toward her. "Out with it. Tell me right now where your truck is. Or am I going to find evidence inside, maybe Philip's blood because he was moved? Where was he when he was shot?"

Something about these two women saying nothing had him feeling as if they were playing with him. He reached for the phone on his desk to start dialing.

"Who are you calling, Mark?" Gail cut in.

He glanced over to Carmen, whose gaze reached out to Gail in a way that said she was somehow a part of this.

"Let's see," he said. "I'm a lone detective on an island where it seems the wife of the chief of police is covering up a crime, confessing to something I know she didn't do. A deputy knows something, surveillance is missing from the camera, and in fact, I'm pretty sure I'm being played. I'm calling the state police."

"Put the phone down, Mark."

He hadn't heard the chief come in. When he turned to the open doorway, he saw fire in the man's eyes. And there too was Cheyenne Potter, who held a brown Manila envelope.

Mark put the phone back in its cradle, and the chief closed the door behind him. Cheyenne was wearing blue jeans and a creamy knit shirt, her hair long and loose, her nose ring glittering.

"I think someone had better start talking and telling me the truth," Mark said.

Cheyenne held out the large brown envelope to him. "This is the legal agreement Philip had me sign. As you'll see in there, it clearly states that I cannot talk about anything of a personal nature that happened between us. I received a total of three hundred thousand dollars to be paid over five years. My aunt did not shoot Philip Maddox. She was trying to protect me…"

"Cheyenne, no! Do not say another word," Gail said. She had started walking toward Cheyenne, but Mark stepped in front of her.

"I will park you in a cell, Gail, if I have to," he said, letting his meaning sink in. He wondered if Gail had been thinking he wouldn't really put everything into this investigation, that he'd just wrap it up and let her go down for it. Evidently, she didn't know him that well.

"Cheyenne, did you shoot Philip?" he asked, still standing in front of Gail. He looked over to Cheyenne and the chief, who motioned for her to continue.

"He came into my shop," Cheyenne said. "He found out I was talking to you, Detective, and that social worker. He figured he had every right to put his hands on me, as he put it, saying he'd paid for me. I knew then that this would never stop with him. He reminded me of the agreement I'd signed, saying he could destroy me and take everything I owned and ever would own, because he was completely, one hundred percent protected by the agreement—even though I knew he was doing it again, this time to his daughter. So I called him…"

"Cheyenne," Gail cut in, a warning. The chief had walked over to his wife and was standing beside her.

Cheyenne only shook her head. "No, Gail, I can't let you do this," she said. "I called him and had him meet me down at the hidden cove he used to take me to when I was sixteen. When he stepped out of his car and walked down to where I was standing, waiting on the rocky shore, I pulled out the gun and I shot him twice. I knew there was no way to stop him and that my cousin would never come forward. He'd keep getting away with it, and I had no legal footing because he had that piece of paper signed by me. He would have my accusation thrown out of court and prevent me from coming forward and testifying against him. I called Gail first, then my mom…"

"Cheyenne, stop talking."

She shook her head again. "Gail, I'm sorry. I shouldn't have listened. I was scared. Gail showed up, and we put Philip in the back of her truck. Mom told me to get in my Jeep, go home and clean up, and Gail took the gun with her. But I don't care what happens to me now, because for the first time I don't have to pretend or be held hostage by that man. For the first time in so long, I feel free of the hold he had on me. Because with him dead, that contract he made me sign is no longer valid."

Mark took in the family—the chief, Gail, and Cheyenne—and Carmen, who'd said not a word. "I need to know where your truck is, Gail," he finally said.

"It's parked out front of our house," the chief answered, holding the keys out to him.

Mark didn't know what to make of the way the man was looking at him. He took the keys and tossed them on his desk, then gestured to Cheyenne. "Put your bag on my desk. You're under arrest, Cheyenne, for the murder of Philip Maddox." Again, he read the Miranda rights, taking in the way she stood there so stoically. "You understand the rights I've read you?"

She only nodded, then looked up to him. "I do. So now can I call a lawyer?"

He picked up the phone on his desk and held it out to her. "Please do, Cheyenne. And take that part seriously. Do not talk to me again without your lawyer."

Chapter 16

There was something strange about showing up at Mark's because he needed her to check in on Lucky, and having the key to his place because he'd told her to take it and keep it. It seemed they were morphing into something that shouldn't have felt this easy.

She closed the door of her brand-new Nissan, taking in the older cottage Mark rented, knowing he was dealing with some pretty heavy shit that she was still trying to wrap her head around.

The murder of a monster.

She had to remind herself that it wasn't okay for someone to take the law into her own hands. But when a man could use the law to protect his crimes… She wondered when it had become so easy to use a contract to cover up a crime. In reality, how much had the law become a tool to silence victims who should never be silenced?

She stepped up on the wide wooden deck, knowing the cooked burgers were still inside the barbecue, now cold and inedible. She took in the old worn plastic deck chairs, then shoved the key in the handle and unlocked the door, hearing the dog jump down off the sofa and come wagging out to her.

Just then, she heard the sound of a vehicle.

She hadn't expected Mark back so soon, and she left the door open, knowing Lucky had wandered outside. She reached for the red wine in the glass on the counter that she hadn't finished and lifted it to take a swallow.

"Oh, you are such a cutie!"

She heard the voice and felt the knot in her stomach.

"Mark, are you here?" Sybil called out. "I didn't see your Jeep, and…"

Billy Jo turned from the sink and took in the tall, slender blonde, her skintight jeans, her long legs. She reminded herself she'd never be the kind of hottie Mark gravitated to. Sybil was staring at her, and Billy Jo was still holding her wine. She pulled her other arm over her stomach, leaning back against the sink, feeling the comfort of her wide cotton capris and bulky loose T-shirt of the Cookie Monster wearing a Christmas hat. Her outfit was built for comfort, not seduction.

"Oh, hey there. Billy Jo, right?" Sybil said after letting out a sharp breath. Her long blond hair was styled straight, her makeup flawless, and her smile displayed perfect straight white teeth. "Is Mark here?"

Billy Jo didn't move, just gestured outside with her wine glass. "Nope, he's working. Was he expecting you?" She knew the way she said it sounded accusing, and the expression on Sybil's face was priceless as she lingered in the doorway. Billy Jo didn't invite her in.

"No, just wanted to talk to him about something, a situation he's helping me with. He's so thoughtful, but you know that, you and Mark being friends and all. So you're here waiting for him?" There it was, the cat claws, the digging.

"Nope, not waiting for him. I'm just finishing a glass of wine, and Lucky and I are hanging out. Again, I can let him know you came by, but not sure when he's going to be back."

Lucky brushed past Sybil in the doorway as he walked back in, and Billy Jo dropped her gaze to the dog and then back to the woman she knew was trying to work her way back into Mark's life.

"You know, Sybil, Mark told me about the jam you're in with the chief's brother," she said, and she didn't miss the way her smile faltered. "I'm sorry you're being harassed. No one should ever have to deal with a man who treats her like that. It has to be scary, especially knowing he's managed to get away with it and keep doing it. But I think you know Mark means what he says in everything. He's as flawed as all of us, but he does live and die by his word. If the chief's brother keeps at you, Mark will do something."

Sybil only nodded, then glanced away and rested her hand on the doorframe. "Yes, he is a good man. I know that intimately well. Does Mark share everything with you? Are you two…?"

Billy Jo wondered why she was still pushing this, but the anger that usually flared within her didn't this time. Sybil dragged her gaze over Billy Jo, from her bare feet in flat comfortable sandals upward, her expression puzzled, leaving the question open.

Lucky wandered over to her and sat beside her, panting, and she ran her hand over his head. She didn't want to discuss anything about her and Mark and what they were with each other, especially not with Sybil. It wasn't her business.

"Sybil, there's a mutual respect between Mark and me—and, well, he was worried about you. Whatever happened between you and Mark before, he's still a cop first, and he doesn't turn his back on someone who needs help. It's hard for a woman when a man can do whatever he wants and you realize you can't do a damn thing to stop him. Keep your head up and stand your ground."

She heard a vehicle, and so did the dog, the familiar hum of Mark's Jeep.

"Speak of the devil," she said. "There he is."

Sybil turned in the doorway, and Billy Jo could hear Mark outside, saying something to the dog, fussing over him. Sybil stepped out on the deck, and Mark called out, "Sybil, everything all right?"

She should walk out there, but instead she just held her wine and took another swallow, hearing his footsteps on the deck. Whatever Sybil said to him, she couldn't make it out. Then there he was in the doorway, walking in, those blue eyes filled with the heaviness of what she knew was on his plate.

She could see that her moody, arrogant detective was stuck in his head. He strode right to her where she leaned against the counter, took in the wine she was holding, and yanked open the fridge to reach for a beer.

"You been here long?" he said.

She shrugged. "Just got here. You done, or do you have to go back?"

He tipped back the bottle and downed half of it, and Sybil was still standing in the doorway, awkward. From the look he gave her, she knew there was so much more going on than what she knew. He leaned against the counter right beside her, holding his beer, and glanced to her and shook his head. Then he looked over to Sybil, who was pulling at her bag in front of her, a smile pasted to her face.

"So he hasn't bothered you again?" Mark said.

"No, he hasn't," Sybil replied. "I guess I just wanted to stop in and say thank you for actually doing something." She gestured toward him, and Billy Jo wondered from the frown on Mark's face whether he had picked up on what she was really doing.

He was standing so close to her, and then he nudged her and said, "You're staying for a bit, right?"

She took in her wine and didn't miss the hopeful look on Sybil's face as Mark waited for her to answer. "Of course I am," she said.

His gaze lingered for just a moment.

"Well, you know what?" Sybil said. "I didn't mean to intrude. I guess you two are…"

Mark settled his beer on the counter behind him and reached over to slide his hand over Billy Jo's arm. "I'm going to grab a quick shower," he said, and she nodded. "Call me at the station, Sybil, if you do have any more problems with Rolly."

Then Mark walked away into his bedroom, and Billy Jo stayed where she was, pretty sure it was disbelief she was seeing in Sybil's expression.

"Well, I guess I should leave you two to your evening," Sybil said.

Billy Jo nodded and put down her glass of wine as she heard the shower pop on.

"Do you mind if I ask you something?" Sybil said.

Billy Jo shrugged. What was she supposed to say? "Sure, what is it?"

"How did you get him to do that?"

She wasn't sure she understood. She shook her head. "Do what…?"

"Look at you like that? Care like that?" Sybil lifted her hands in front of her and stepped back in the doorway. "You know what? Don't answer that," she said. Then she lifted her hand in a wave, and Billy Jo heard her walking across the deck.

Then there was the sound of a car door, the engine starting, and she just stood there in the quietness, hearing the water running in the shower as Sybil pulled away.

She had realized that here with Mark was the only place she wanted to be.

Mark listened to the rustling in the kitchen after standing under the hot spray for what had seemed like forever. When he strode out in nothing more than a clean pair of jeans, barefoot and bare chested, his hair damp, he realized Billy Jo was outside at the barbecue, cooking another burger.

He took in the dried-up ones she must have pulled off the barbecue, sitting on a plate in the sink, then reached for the beer he hadn't finished and walked to the door. He leaned against the doorframe, looking out to where his Jeep was parked beside her car.

Her gaze landed on his chest, then likely on the tattoo of a woman he couldn't believe he still had to look at every day.

She didn't smile. In fact, she held the spatula out to him and said, "You can finish this. Figured you were hungry."

He reached for the spatula, seeing two burgers on the grill. "You know I plan on having it removed," he said. He listened to the creak of the plastic chair on the deck.

"Having what removed, Mark?"

He turned to her as she reached for her wine glass on the small wooden table that had always been on this deck. "The tattoo."

She said nothing at first, watching him as if she didn't know how to respond. "So what happened at the station? Gail, what's going to happen to her? Did you hear from the DA?"

Mark flipped the burgers and took in the flicker of the fire, then pulled in a heavy breath, still pissed over what had felt like one big secret. "Well, the shitshow evolved. Imagine my surprise when Cheyenne showed up with the chief and confessed to shooting Philip. I honestly don't know what the hell Gail was thinking. It seems Carmen knew something about it, too, so I feel like I was the only one in the dark. I can't figure out whether they thought there was a way to pull the strings from the background while I was running this investigation or that I wouldn't actually do my job and investigate."

He turned back to Billy Jo, taking in her wide eyes. By the way her jaw slackened and she looked away, he was pretty sure she couldn't think of what to say.

"What the hell, Mark? Why?"

"Do you want me to try to guess why Gail would throw herself in the line of fire and play roulette with the possibility of prison time for a crime she confessed to? She's furious because she didn't do something to stop Philip. Then there's Carmen, who knew about the staged scene and said nothing, and so did the chief. I'm pretty sure one of them also washed out the blood from Gail's truck. Oh, yeah. Did I forget to mention that part? They moved his body—Gail, her sister, and Cheyenne, that is.

"Or do you want to hear that Cheyenne killed him, Philip, in pre-meditated cold blood because she wanted to be free of the piece of paper that prevented her from talking? Cheyenne held that secret for so long that she knew he'd keep getting away with it. Even after I told her to talk only to her lawyer, she told me that she felt as if a weight had been lifted from her for the first time, because now nothing's preventing her from talking, from telling everyone what he did. The only problem now is how many people are part of the crime and are going to have to face consequences."

At least it was now in the hands of the DA. The confession had been handled, and Gail and the chief's roles would have to be sorted out. Then there were Carmen and Cheyenne's mother.

Billy Jo glanced down to her hands, holding her wine, and tilted her head subtly as she said, "You know what, Mark? She's right."

The way she said it, he really looked at her. "Who's right, Cheyenne or Gail?"

Billy Jo shook her head. "Look, I like Gail, and maybe I'm a little in her corner because she did something to stop a monster. Maybe you don't get it, but knowing that man did what he did to Cheyenne, I understand, Mark. Because I've lived it. The worst is knowing he's going to keep getting away with it. I can honestly say if I was in her shoes, I may have done the same thing. Remember, she couldn't talk about it, so he'd keep doing it. Men like him keep getting away with it until someone is brave enough to do something…"

"You mean like Cheyenne did?" He couldn't believe she'd suggested it. "You're talking an eye for an eye, Billy Jo, and the law has no room for that." Mark turned off the gas and watched the flame flicker out.

"Am I? I thought I was talking about stopping him. Don't forget he had the law on his side."

"You mean the signed nondisclosure?"

Billy Jo rested her wine on the side table and stood up. She stepped over to him and stopped right beside him, looking at the burgers and then up to him. "You asked me to open up. When you're a kid, you shouldn't have to worry that someone you should be able to trust is hurting you. The first time it happened to me, I was eleven. He was a social worker approaching retirement. When he touched me at first, I froze. The next time, I couldn't believe it was happening.

"He always promised me something, or if I didn't comply, he'd tell me he might have to move me to a new home. Fear is a powerful motivator. The thing is, Mark, there's a lot of this that I don't want in my own head. I've had to come to terms with it, but even though I didn't have a nondisclosure that prevented me from talking, it felt like I did, because I wasn't believed. I did not have a voice. He managed my file. He wrote down that I lied, that I ran, that I was angry, violent, fucked up already. And, worse, he told me he'd done that." Her arms were pulled over her chest, and she looked down at the burgers.

He wanted to kill the man who'd done that to her.

She flicked her gaze up to him. "I never told my dad about him," she said, and the way she was looking at him, he realized what she was trusting him with.

"Is he still alive?" he said.

She made a face and shook her head. "No."

He didn't know why he was furious about that. "Good," he said, "because I seriously hope someone killed him slowly and painfully."

She ran her hand over his arm, taking in the woman he'd tattooed there after too many beers and a giant heartache. "So when are you planning on having that taken off? Because I have to tell you, I'm not interested in seeing the face of your former girlfriend every time you walk around without your shirt on."

He nodded. "I'll call tomorrow, make an appointment for next week."

She walked back into his cabin and stopped in the doorway, where she looked back to him, her gaze lingering on his chest, an odd smile on her lips. "Well, now," she said. "That sounds like a great place to start."

Chapter 17

M ark's phone was ringing. He didn't know when he'd finally fallen asleep, but now he jerked awake, and his hand went to the phone as he blinked in the early morning light. He pressed the green answer icon. "Yeah, what?" was all he could get out, his throat groggy. His hand went to his forehead as he lay there and shut his eyes again.

"Detective Friessen, this is Mary Jane Trundell with the town council."

Mark was sitting up now, blinking. The dog was at the foot of the bed, his head on Mark's foot. He slid out from under the covers and sat up, his feet on the cool hardwood floor. It was only five thirty in the morning.

"Are you there, Detective?"

"Yeah, sorry, I was asleep. Why are you calling?" He cleared his throat and ran his hand over his face as the dog jumped off the bed and shook. Mark leaned his forearms on his bare legs and took in the empty other side of his bed, then stood up, stretching.

"The council called an emergency meeting last night

about the chief and Gail Shephard and the shooting of Philip Maddox. This is going to be a nightmare because of who he is. The council has already voted that you're to be interim chief while the investigation plays out."

Now he was wide awake. He strode out to the kitchen in just his boxer briefs and reached for the coffeepot. "Me? You want me to be chief. Does the chief know this?"

Maybe he'd have thought of something different to say if he hadn't still been half asleep. He put his cell phone on speaker and filled the coffeepot with water.

"We need you to go over to Tolly Shephard's and notify him. The council is searching for his replacement, but again, in the meantime, Detective, you're being appointed interim chief. You're to oversee the department and make sure this investigation doesn't turn into a three-ring circus. The DA has already reached out, and until the Shephards' involvement in the shooting of Mr. Maddox is resolved, the chief will have to step down…"

From the way she was talking, Mark thought something else was playing out behind the scenes and someone else was directing it. "Look, Ms. Trundell, let me be very clear here. This is an active investigation, and I seriously hope you aren't under the impression you can tell me how to run it. I'll be talking to the DA this morning…"

"Detective Friessen, I've already spoken with the DA. In fact, Melanie Kramer has taken the lead on this and was part of the council meeting last night."

He stared at the cupboard, the wood front, and wondered what the hell was going on. "Excuse me, why is the DA speaking with you?"

"Detective Friessen, Philip Maddox is the political consultant and strategist to Mr. Fitzpatrick."

Mark shoved the carafe on the burner, not sure he'd heard her right. "We're not talking about Senator Fitzpatrick, are we?" Yup, he was wide awake now.

"The very same. So imagine what's coming down on this office, on the DA. Those late-night phone calls were the reason for our emergency meeting. This isn't some average Joe who was killed, and Fitzpatrick's office has already reached out, demanding answers. Don't watch the news, because this is going to be all over it. The chief is going to disappear, out of the spotlight, and no one is to talk to the media. I understand someone from the senator's office will reach out to tell you what you can and can't say."

Mark stared down at his cell phone, on speaker, feeling that noose being slipped around him as he was handled again. Maybe that was why he was feeling uneasy. "This is sounding like the senator's office is expecting to be kept updated on every aspect of this case or to run the investigation. Or is it that they're looking for this to be shut down quietly with a certain outcome? Surely you know about the allegations concerning Philip Maddox. I wouldn't want to be the senator right now, associated with him, after what he's been accused of…"

"That's the reason we're talking now," she said, cutting him off.

Mark reached for the grounds and dumped them in the basket, then flicked the switch to turn the coffeemaker on.

"The DA has already agreed that Philip Maddox, who is now dead and can't defend himself against allegations, will not go on trial. Anything said about him is unfounded and will probably be inadmissible."

What?

Mark dragged his hand over his face again, hearing the scrape of whiskers.

"Everyone wants this quietly put to bed," she continued, "especially the council. So you go and see Tolly Shephard to notify him he's off the job and you'll be taking over. The council will issue a statement that he's stepped down for personal reasons, and the senator's office will be looking for an update."

Mark was already shaking his head. "I don't answer to the senator or his office, and I'm not having an investigation silenced because it doesn't look good."

"No, but you answer to the council, Detective, and we expect an update by the end of the day." Then she hung up.

Mark took in his cell phone and breathed in the brewing coffee. "Shit…" he said under his breath.

The dog was sitting at the door, waiting to go out. He walked over and unlocked it, seeing the hint of pink in the sky as the sunrise popped on the horizon. He left the door open as he pulled up his contacts and dialed, then heard the ring and the groggy "What!"

"It's Mark. You awake?" He could hear rustling in the background.

"You're kidding, right? It's, like, not even six. Are you crazy, calling this early?"

Mark reached for a mug in the dish drain, seeing it was clean, and poured a coffee. "Just got a call from the council. I have to go pay the chief a visit and let him know I'm now filling in for him. Did you know Philip Maddox was a political advisor for Senator Fitzpatrick's office? Apparently there was some late-night emergency meeting, and, by the sounds of it, they're trying to shut down anything that could come back on the senator. According to Mary Jane Trundell, who called me, by the way, the DA has stated that Philip Maddox won't be on trial, and…"

"You're being handled," Billy Jo cut in.

He was already nodding as he walked to the open door, watching the dog wandering in the overgrown grass. "Yeah, figured as much. So, any guesses on how this is going to play out? I mean, as you said, your father is or was—"

"Probably one of the best legal minds out there, and he was the best fixer of problems in Washington. Basically, you'll give all your evidence and charges to the DA, who will decide who to prosecute, what to prosecute, and what we can investigate. My guess is there's no way in hell the senator will want his office linked in any way to a child molester, so you can bet they're in damage control mode right now, coming up with a spin to protect the senator. The first order of business is to make sure it doesn't get out.

"You won't get a call, but your boss's boss has already been notified, and deals are already under way. A news story about some other tragedy is likely already in the works to take the spotlight off this. But you should know that if the story can't be contained, it may suddenly come to light that the senator's office had notified the Feds, who have secretly been investigating the Roche Harbor police for hiding and protecting a sexual predator. If there happens to be any fallout on you, they won't protect you. Is that what you want to hear, Mark?"

She was damn smart, and he realized she was his

go-to.

He winced. "No, but that's what I thought." He took in the early morning and the silence, and for a moment, he wished she were there.

Baby steps, that voice in his head reminded him.

"What are you going to do?"

He only shook his head. "I'm going to finish my coffee, grab a shower, and pay the chief a visit. Beyond that, I guess I'll have to see who's waiting in the office when I go in."

The dog was wandering in the bushes now, and he could just make out his tail.

"Some advice?" she said.

From her? Anything. "Sure."

"Listen only," she said. "Don't commit to anything. And if your phone just happens to be on and recording, consider that your insurance so something won't suddenly come back on you."

The dog now trotted back onto the deck.

Mark took a swallow of his steaming coffee. "Dinner tonight?" he said. He heard rustling again in the background, and he pictured her in her apartment, alone with her cat.

"How about we stay in?" she said. "You can come here tonight, and that way you'll make yourself unavailable to anyone who wants to stop by and ask you about what happened."

He nodded. "See you tonight," he said, then held his disconnected phone, thinking of the only girl he trusted with his life.

He needed to see the chief now, and he wondered how right Billy Jo would be about what awaited him when he walked into the station that day.

Chapter 18

A blue pickup and a red Subaru were parked out front of the chief's along with Gail's truck and the chief's police cruiser. Mark knew it was early, and the sun had just come up as he walked past Gail's Tacoma. The inside was clean, freshly detailed.

He had his badge tucked into his jeans, his sunglasses on, and his gun holstered as he went to the door, listened to the quiet, and rang the bell, which chimed inside. He waited before hearing footsteps on the stairs, and then the door opened.

Gail, whom he hadn't expected to see, wore a long nightgown with a sweater pulled overtop, and her hair was a mess. "Mark, you're here early."

He wasn't sure she'd invite him in as she stood in the doorway. He lifted his sunglasses and rested them on top of his head in his thick red hair. "I need to speak to the chief."

Gail ran her hand over her face. She'd walked out with her lawyer the day before because the ADA, Kyle

Ladner, had shown up and said to let her go and charge Cheyenne.

Then there were Carmen and the chief. He'd sit down today with the DA, but he already suspected he might not like what he was going to hear.

She nodded and looked past him. "You didn't bring Lucky?"

He made a face as he stepped inside. "Not today. So how are you?"

He had expected something other than what he saw in her expression. She shut her eyes and gave her head a shake, and he realized how tired she looked.

"You know I'm not supposed to be talking to you," she said, then reached over and ran her hand over his arm. "Tolly is out back. He's expecting you."

Of all things, he hadn't expected that. She closed the door behind him, and he started to the kitchen, taking in the open French doors. He spotted the chief sitting on a red cushioned patio set on the back lawn, looking out to the ocean. It was a spectacular view.

Mark glanced back to see that Gail was now gone. He listened to footsteps on the stairs and took one step, then another toward the dining table, where the chief's gun and badge were. He picked up the badge but put it down before walking out and down the steps off the deck, onto the lawn, over to the chief, who didn't turn around.

Mark headed for the second padded chair but just stood there for a second, looking down at the chief, who held an empty mug.

"Badge and gun are on the table," the chief said.

Mark only nodded, squinting in the morning sun,

but he didn't put his sunglasses back on. "So you were expecting me?"

The chief looked up to him, and he wasn't sure what he saw there. "You're taking over, Mark, and the DA will not be pursuing Gail. That was my agreement to step down."

Mark glanced at the chair and didn't wait for an invite before he sat down, taking in the view the chief was gazing out at. "You know what bothers me out of all this, chief? Gail's sister was married to that man, and now a young woman's life is ruined because no one did anything. Did Cheyenne really tell her mother, and she did nothing?"

He wondered how a mother could do that to her daughter. If she'd come forward years ago, they wouldn't be there now.

"There was a group of us who fished with Philip every Saturday in the summer. We'd take his boat out on the water. He made a call once when our daughter Lori found herself in deep water on a trip down in Texas with a bunch of her friends when she was twenty. He yanked her out unscathed. He's also responsible for two in the group, the CEOs of tech corporations, winning government contracts worth billions for planning, construction, consulting, and management with some agency in the Department of Defense. Doing what, I'm not exactly sure…" The chief lifted his hand, then dropped it.

"So Philip Maddox was pretty important," Mark said. "You have any idea what I can expect? You know Maddox did some horrible things, and there's that contract Cheyenne had to sign…"

"It can't be used, Mark. She may have thought

killing him would let her talk, but I already know she can't. My son Richard stayed over last night, upstairs, and Graham called and told me to talk to Trish, my youngest, in Paris. She called me back at four this morning. She's not coming back. She said she knew about Philip because when she was fourteen, we were over at their house for Thanksgiving, and he had her downstairs alone."

Mark just stared in horror.

The chief appeared so thrown. He cleared his throat and shook his head before looking over to Mark. "She said she told him to stop, and he did, and she never told us."

Mark realized what he was seeing in the man's expression: anger, rage, blame.

"Cheyenne will have the best lawyer provided for her," the chief continued. "No one wants this to come out. The story will be something else, and if there's a trial, she'll be acquitted. But my guess is that it won't go that far, because no one wants the dirty laundry of our family hanging for the world to see."

Mark wanted to argue with the chief. "And Cheyenne's mother, who did nothing when she told her?"

The chief wouldn't look his way, only shook his head. "Gail and her sisters have a complicated relationship, but what I do know is that to them, family is everything. They protect their own. Evidently, Patrice turning a blind eye to what Philip did was easier than saying it had happened. He was doing it to his youngest daughter, too. Cheyenne was right. Bev now knows, but no one in her family will talk about it. Philip will get his funeral."

Mark didn't know what to say. He thought this was

the first time words had failed to form in his mind. "Chief, this isn't right. He needs to be exposed. How many other girls did he do this to?"

The chief looked right at him. "Does it matter? He's dead now. Pretty sure justice has been served."

Mark just stared at the man he'd worked under and butted heads with. He knew he'd never understand how a family could look away. "You know, Chief, if that were my child and I found out, I'd have killed him."

The chief looked at him with a hard, unsmiling gaze.

"You gave Cheyenne the gun," Mark said.

The chief pulled in a breath and looked away, then flicked his hand back toward the house. "They'll try to replace you with someone else, Mark. Don't let them. Stand your ground and hire your own replacement. When the council calls you and you have to sit before them every week and report on crimes, on what you're doing, they'll try to tell you how to run your department and who to let off. Pull aside Herb Walker, who always sits right beside Mary Jane, and tell him you know about the cut he's still taking from the budget set aside for the island's homeless. Tell Hal Green you have a copy of all the tickets he insisted I write off. And tell Mary Jane, who was sleeping with Philip Maddox, that photos of her walking into the Hilton suite in Portland are in your bottom drawer. They'll leave you alone."

Mark wasn't sure what expression was on his face as he angled his head. "I'm not blackmailing anyone."

The chief didn't nod, didn't smile. "I figured you'd say that. You're too good for this job, Mark. But let me give you some advice. The fact is that the council here, the Feds, the senator, and Gail's family, as well as everyone who received a contract or benefit from Philip, all have a vested interest in preventing the truth from coming out. You're not dealing with just one person or one organization. Don't forget he had friends who reaped contracts worth billions. But, being chief here, if you're smart, you can make some things right, one at a time, quietly, holding your cards to your chest. You understand?"

Mark figured this was one of the times Billy Jo talked about where he needed to shut his mouth and say nothing. He stood up.

The chief lifted his hand again. "Badge and gun. Take them on your way out. And in the bottom drawer of my desk is everything I told you about. Here's the key. Use it or don't." The chief had pulled a set of keys from his pocket and held them out to Mark, and he took them and stuffed them into his pocket.

"If you need anything…" Mark started to say.

The chief only lifted his hand to stop him. "You leave Carmen alone, too. She only followed orders. She's had a rough road, and trust doesn't come easy to her. But you know she'll always have your back."

Mark didn't say anything, just started walking back to the house, up onto the deck, and through the open French doors. He reached for the badge and gun, took in the quiet inside, and kept right on walking out the front door.

Chapter 19

"Did you hear that hot detective of yours is the new chief of police?" Pam said, poking her head into the office where Billy Jo had been typing up a report on her laptop.

She looked over, seeing the expression on Pam's face, and for a second she thought she was kidding.

"I take it you haven't heard?" Pam said.

How the hell was she supposed to reply to that? She stared over at Pam, who was all smiles. Billy Jo knew she had been the one to open her mouth about Cheyenne showing up at their office. There was just something about the woman that she'd never trusted.

"And you heard this from…?" She finished uploading the Word doc to her email and sent it to Grant, then closed the laptop and turned her chair.

"It's all over town. Well, I heard it from Merv, who runs the tavern and restaurant at the Dixie hotel by the ferry, who heard it from Charles at the gas station, who heard it from…"

"Okay, got it." Billy Jo held up the flat of her hand.

"Thanks, Pam, for the update." She turned back to her laptop.

"Well, aren't you going to call him?"

Billy Jo pulled in a breath and shook her head, wondering what in all hell had happened as a result of him filling in for the chief. She wondered why he hadn't called. But she resisted the urge to pick up her cell phone and see if she'd missed it.

"Pam, if this is true, then he's likely really busy, so no, I'm not going to bug him. I'll talk to him later."

Pam looked at her like a little kid who hadn't gotten her favorite toy. As soon as she stepped back and walked to her desk, Billy Jo reached for her cell phone. Nope, nothing from Mark. She took in the clock on the wall, seeing it was just after lunch, so she reached for her baggy purse, tossed her phone in it, slung it over her shoulder, and walked out of the office.

"I'm going out for a sandwich. Can I bring you anything?" she called out to Pam, who was back behind her desk, as she headed for the door.

"Nope, but say hi to the detective for me."

Billy Jo froze for a second, her hand on the lock, before she flicked it open and glanced over her shoulder to Pam, who had a bright smile. Okay, so she couldn't just slip out.

"Fine," was all she said as she opened the door. She relocked it behind her and climbed into her car, where she hesitated for only a second, wondering if maybe this wasn't a good time to show up at the station. But this was Mark, and if the roles were reversed, she knew he'd have shown up and asked her why she couldn't pick up the phone.

As she drove down the main street, she spotted the

café they'd both avoided for so long, and she found herself pulling in. Mark probably hadn't eaten, so what was the harm in grabbing a couple of sandwiches before she went to the station?

She stepped out of her car, feeling a smile tugging at her lips, before she spotted a council notice taped to the door, an order of closure. She thought she saw someone inside, so she put her hand on the knob and turned. When she stepped inside the empty café, Sybil was loading up a basket with supplies.

"I'm closed," Sybil called out without looking her way.

"I see that. Why? And what is that, posted on your door?"

Sybil walked the basket over to a table and lifted her hands. Her blond hair, usually neat and tidy, was pulled back in a messy bun, and there were sweat stains under the arms of her peach T-shirt. Billy Jo knew when someone was emotionally gutted.

"Seems Rolly got his wish," Sybil said. "Showed up this morning to find a surprise visit from a health inspector, who officially shut me down. He walked through my place and said a complaint had been filed against me about several health violations. Said I don't have proper refrigeration, I don't have the proper labeling for expired foods, my signage isn't up to code, there's improper storage of cleaning supplies… Here's the checklist he completed. Everything on there is bullshit. Then he taped the closure notice on my door. He had his mind made up before he came in here…

She handed the paper to Billy Jo, who took in the notes and violations, issues she'd have expected from a cockroach-infested greasy spoon, not Sybil's neat and tidy café.

"You'll have to fight this, Sybil. This isn't okay. You should let Mark know."

Sybil let out a rough sigh and shook her head. "You know, I built this place from nothing, but as long as I stay here, the chief's brother will always be a problem."

Bill Jo slid her gaze from the violation checklist up to her. Sybil really was beautiful.

"No, I'm done," she continued. "My brother owns a restaurant in Olympia, and he's been bugging me to come down there and help him out. I think this is the writing on the wall for me. I want some peace. If I stay here and fight this, sure, I'll win eventually, but at what cost?" She shook her head.

Billy Jo took in the wrapped sandwiches, scones, and cookies stuffed into a container, everything boxed up and bagged. "And what about all your food?"

Sybil shrugged. "Was going to take it over to Charles down at the gas station. He knows a lot of families struggling. I'm sure he'll see to it that it's not wasted."

Billy Jo reached for her wallet and pulled out a fifty. "Here. I'll take four of whatever you have."

She took in the hesitation before Sybil reached for a paper bag stuffed in a box on the counter and shoved sandwiches, cookies, and a couple cinnamon buns into it. She handed it to Billy Jo, offering her a tight smile. "Thank you."

Billy Jo only nodded, taking the bag, and turned to leave.

"Can I ask you something?"

She turned back. The way Sybil knit her brows

together, she sensed the question might be one she didn't want to answer, so she said nothing.

"Mark. I always knew deep down he had a thing for you. I guess what I need to know is what you have to give him that I don't."

She didn't know how to answer. She stared at this sexy, hot girl she knew guys gravitated to, and she shrugged. "I don't know what it is exactly, but I'd trust him with my life, I can talk to him about anything, and he makes me happy."

Sybil shook her head and pasted on a tight smile. "Thanks for stopping by," she said.

Billy Jo pulled open the door, glancing once more at the health notice taped there, and climbed into her car with the bag of sandwiches.

She drove the block to the station, seeing Marks's Jeep out front with two other cars, along with Carmen's cruiser. She climbed out and opened the door to the station to find the phone ringing, Carmen talking at her desk, and Mark in the chief's office along with a man in a dark blue suit and a woman in a dress and pumps, who she thought was Mary Jane Trundell, head of the town council.

Carmen hung up the phone and then answered the other line, and Billy Jo took in Gail's empty desk, then Mark's, which appeared neat and tidy. She flicked her gaze to him, seeing he'd spotted her, and lifted the paper bag so he would see it, then sat it on his desk.

Carmen hung up the phone and let out a heavy sigh. "So did you hear?"

Billy Jo walked over to her. "So it's true? Mark is the chief, not just filling in? How did that happen?" she said in a low voice.

She heard Mark talking but couldn't make it out. Carmen glanced once over her shoulder just as Mary Jane and whoever the guy in the suit was walked out, first from the chief's office and then from the station.

"You brought food?" Mark called out. He slapped his hands together, his cowboy boots scraping on the ground.

"Yeah, I picked you up some sandwiches."

He rummaged in the bag and pulled out one to toss to Carmen, who caught it. "Thanks," he said. "I'm starving, and not a chance I'm getting out of here today."

Billy Jo dragged her gaze from Mark to Carmen and back, watching as both bit into the sandwiches she'd brought—ham or salami, she wasn't sure. "Well, is anyone going to tell me what's going on? Is it true you're the official new island chief?"

"Apparently," was all he said between bites. "It's been a morning. Carmen, I'm going to need you to handle the nuisance complaint out at the Tuckers'."

Carmen shoved another bite of the sandwich in her mouth and reached for her keys as she stood up. "Sure, Chief. What about rounds? You want me to keep to the same schedule?"

Mark shook his head. "No, I want you staggering the times. And, Carmen…" He pulled open his drawer and reached for his badge, then tossed it to her. Again, she caught it one handed. "When you come in tomorrow, Detective Zarco, you can leave the uniform at home."

Billy Jo took in her wide eyes as she realized what had happened.

"You're giving me a promotion?"

Mark stared at her with that hard gaze. "You deserve it. Just don't ever lie to me like that again."

Carmen nodded. Billy Jo could see what this meant to her.

"Thanks, Chief," she said, then walked out the door.

That left Billy Jo and Mark.

"So what happened?" she said.

Mark angled his head as he reached into the bag and pulled out a sandwich for her. When she reached for it, his fingers touched hers. "Other than the fact that I'm now officially the chief?" He gestured to the door. "That was the assistant DA. Apparently, since the big news stations haven't gotten hold of this story, they think they can contain it quietly. Cheyenne is taking a deal. She'll get probation, he said. A gift, really, considering."

"And Gail and the chief?" She unwrapped the sandwich, ham and cheese, and took a bite.

Mark shoved the last of his sandwich in his mouth. "Nothing. The chief is officially retiring, and I have to start interviewing for a new deputy this week. The phone has been ringing off the hook, mainly people who've known the chief forever, asking why he left."

Billy Jo took in the office and the man she cared so much for. "Well, you know what, Mark? I, for one, am glad you're the new chief. Do you think it's completely inappropriate, considering the circumstances, if we celebrate?"

He took a bite of a cookie, then put it down on the desk and wiped his hands together. "I think it's a great idea. You know, the chief had a certain way of doing things, and I never realized until I saw him this morning. It wasn't just about policing the island, as I discovered from that visit I had moments ago. The council is trying to handle me, tell me what to police and what not to. I can tell by your face you're not surprised."

What was she supposed to say? That was a world she understood well. During her dad's life in politics, he'd shared so much about how things worked behind the scenes, everything he'd had to fix.

"So are you letting them?" She took another bite.

Mark glanced to the side. There was something so damn attractive about him when he was thinking. When he settled those baby blues back on her, she knew she was sunk. "You think I would let anyone handle me?"

She shook her head and let out a soft laugh. "Well, that's a good thing, Mark. So tell me, when we celebrate tonight, where do you want to go?"

He didn't pull his gaze from her. "Your place. You promised me dinner, remember?" There was that flicker of mischief in his eyes.

"Chief Mark Friessen… How about that? It kind of rolls off the tongue." She really couldn't wait until tonight, because for the first time, she realized he really did have eyes only for her.

Turn the page for a sneak peek of
THE STRANGER AT THE DOOR the next book in the
BILLY JO MCCABE MYSTERY
Available in print, eBook & audio

Next in the Billy Jo McCabe
Mystery

She knocked on his door. He never should have answered.

--"Absolutely chilling."

Rebmay

As newly appointed chief of police, Mark Friessen is settling into his small-town role when he uncovers the twisted tale of a woman forced to marry the man who killed her family.

When the woman goes looking for help, knocking on his door, Mark and Billy Jo are thrust into a web of lies that tests their own complex relationship, as they discover secrets in the couple's shadowy past that could drive a wedge between them for good.

Mark and Billy Jo are continuing to learn the hard way

that stepping on the wrong toes could have serious consequences. Thrown into the center of a dangerous and bizarre case, they have to face their own doubts about each other, and soon, they may wish this woman had never knocked on Mark's door.

"You given any thought to redoing this office and really making it yours? You know, putting your own stamp on it?" Billy Jo was sitting in a padded old chair, her bare feet in flip-flops up on his desk, and he thought she wore pink nail polish on her toes. Something about the bellbottom blue jeans and light peach blouse she wore, which even hinted that she was a girl, had him wondering what was different about her as of late.

He looked around the glassed-in office, with its old desk covered in papers and files, the cabinet behind him, and the computer, and he gestured from where he lounged in the black swivel chair, which had once been the chief's. "It's just an office, Billy Jo, and it is mine. I don't need anything fancy."

She shot him a look from across the desk, where she seemed to fit so well, lounging. They had settled into a routine that was both welcome and expected, with her stopping in after work every day. "Well, at least paint it," she said. "What are all those plaques up there on the wall? Is that a baseball back there? And those old photos, Mark, you've got to take those down." She gestured to them, unsmiling. This was the snarky side of Billy Jo that came out when she had something to say.

He had to fight the urge to smile. She was so familiar. He didn't turn around to see the black and white photos on the wall of the young chief, then a new cop, standing with the old chief he'd later replaced and the council. He'd personally never met any of them. He stood up and reached for one, seeing a smile on the face of the old chief, one he never remembered seeing, and looked over to Billy Jo, taking in her blue eyes. He was doing his damnedest to figure out where to tread with her and how this thing he couldn't put a name to worked between them.

"Fine. I'll box this up, but I'm not painting. You want to do it, be my guest. Since you're just sitting there, take a look at these." He reached for a pile of applications and resumes for the new deputy position and dumped them on the desk in front of her with a *thunk*. In the bullpen outside, Carmen, who wore blue jeans and a faded black T-shirt, was really pulling double duty since they were down to just the two of them. He missed having Gail to answer the phones and do all she had done to keep the station running.

"So what are these?" Billy Jo reached for the pile of papers as she dropped her feet to the ground.

He realized, as he looked at her brown hair, that it appeared the layers had been freshly cut. Something about her seemed so different, so not the girl hiding behind frumpy clothes. He walked around the desk, watching the way she thumbed through the papers, the way her brow knit when she was focused, reading and absorbing something, the way she never hesitated to jump in. She was so damn smart that her opinion on everything mattered to him more than he could have explained to anyone.

"Resumes, applications for the deputy job, someone to answer the phones and do everything Gail did. The top of the pile there was sent over by the council, and see all the ones with a red star marked on top? The council has pretty much ordered me to hire one of them. The ones on the bottom are the ones I found and came across."

She flicked those blue eyes up to him, reading between the lines and knowing what he was thinking without him having to say another word. This was the comfortable relationship they were morphing into.

He kept walking out the open door and over to the corner by Gail's old desk, where a few boxes were stacked for recycling. He took in Lucky, who was curled up, asleep, before he reached for a box and walked back across the bullpen. Carmen was hanging up the phone, and her chair squeaked as she stretched and started closing up files. She lifted her gaze to him, her wary dark eyes tracking him, and he found himself stopping beside her desk.

"You get today's report finished?" he said.

She opened her laptop without a word and gestured to the screen as if she expected him to check her work. He didn't look at her screen, not pulling his gaze from her, still holding the box and waiting, so she pulled in a breath and said, "Was about to email it to you. Theft at the pharmacy of a bunch of back-to-school supplies, some drinking in the park, public indecency, and a lot of nuisance crap that would seem to indicate an alarming rise, except it seems most troublemakers were used to the times Chief Shephard had me run the same route, so that tells me everyone had their watches set to when I would be making the rounds like clockwork, and it was only the idiots who were getting caught. Now I can't drive anywhere without seeing something, and there isn't enough of me going around to do anything. Then there are all the noise complaints, parties, loud music, neighbors fighting, and the bylaw crap still tossed this way, from illegal camping to people living in their cars, and where am I supposed to tell them to go?"

He could see her frustration. "Do what you can. It's a judgement call. Send me the report, and I'll see what I can take off your plate until I get a deputy hired in here."

She sat up and swiveled her chair around. "Well, won't be soon enough for me, Mark—sorry, Chief."

There was something odd about being called Chief. He wondered if he'd ever get used to it.

"Clock out and go have some dinner," he said. "I'm going to be here awhile yet."

Carmen yanked her desk drawer open and pulled out her keys, and Mark walked back to his office, where Billy Jo was reading through the stack of applications. Damn, she was too perfect. He had to remind himself how easily he could sabotage the good things in his life.

"You look nice, in case I forgot to mention it," he said as he rested the box on his desk. "You did something new with your hair."

She suddenly stilled. Right, she didn't take compliments at all. From the way she flicked those sharp blue eyes to him, he could tell she was uncomfortable, and he waited for her to toss something snarky his way.

"Here. You picked the ones on the bottom?" she said. Okay, so she was going to ignore the compliment. That was one way not to handle it. She pulled out two papers and held them out to him, and he reached for them, seeing two names, Mike Schneider and Georgette Hunter.

"That was quick," he said. "Why these two and not the starred ones favored by the council?"

She neatened the pile of papers and then leaned back in the chair, balancing them on her lap. "Well, for one, it would take a fool not to see that of the council picks, most are either their friends or relatives or, as with these first two, have more experience than you, so the council is likely looking for your replacement, someone who is going to do exactly what they say, report to them, and take all their directions directly. I happen to know that after every weekly meeting you have with the councillors, a few of them criticize you, complaining and commenting that you're going to ruin the policing on the island."

He stared at her as he pulled the black and whites off the wall and tucked them into the box. "Excuse me?" he said. What was she hearing that he wasn't? She didn't even smile, and he could see she was dead serious. "Are you shitting me? Who in all hell is talking out of turn? What goes on in the council is confidential, yet now you're telling me…"

"You're stepping on toes, Mark."

He straightened and could feel the alpha fighting inside him. His first instinct as he took in the seriousness staring back at him was to walk out the door and knock on the door of the head of council, Mary Jane Trundell, or maybe Hal Green or Herb Walker, so he could go toe to toe with them and find out what the fuck they thought they were doing, sharing anything about what went on in the council.

"I can tell by your face that you're ready to go a round with one or all of them," she said, "but that would be a mistake. I'm not sure how many are furious, but I know Herb Walker has been the most vocal, and I heard Hal Green was talking about how you don't play ball with the Rotary Club. Several have said Mary Jane isn't happy with you and the fact that you're going all cowboy with your policing." She lifted the stack and settled them on his desk as she leaned forward.

His jaw slackened as he rested both hands on the edge of the box and squeezed, then lifted his hand and dragged it over his jaw roughly. "Are you sure? They said I was a cowboy, seriously? Is that because I outright refused to allow the council to dictate to me which crimes to ignore and which to put my focus on? Did you know we currently have more than three dozen people sleeping in their cars on the island because they can't put a roof over their head? The council has ordered me to make sure they know they can't park anywhere overnight, which means basically kicking them off the island.

"Then we had three driving without a license. One was a young mother who couldn't have afforded bail or the license renewal fee, and I knew that, so I let her off with a warning and told her to park and pay the fee, but the council ordered me to charge her and lock her up. If I do, she won't get out until she goes before a judge, and then she'll be hit with another fine she won't be able to afford, so she'll still be locked up, and her kids will be tossed in the social services system.

"Of the other two I stopped, one shithead had lost his license for driving two times over the legal limit, and he refused a breathalyzer, yet his lawyer had him out before the ink was dry, citing that he was on pain meds and wasn't drinking. That was a load of crap, considering the alcohol on his breath could have knocked me over. He just so happens to be a cousin of Herb Walker.

"The other was a snotnosed teenager who took his mom's BMW for a joy ride. The family is from Seattle, and the dad is some tech giant with a summer home here worth millions. You know that kid laughed when Carmen pulled him over? He'd almost run down an elderly woman on one of those mobility scooters. When Carmen yanked him out of the car, he screamed at her to keep her dirty half-breed hands off him and said his dad would make sure she was fired and would pay for it."

Billy Jo said nothing. Mark had refused to back down when it came to how the council felt they could tell him to police this island: kid gloves with some and paramilitary tactics with others.

"Yeah, I heard about that too," she said with a hint of a smile. "Wasn't it Mary Jane whose phone was ringing with a call from the dad, who apparently contributed largely to her campaign? He threatened that he had enough clout to redirect infrastructure funding from the island to another region and halt the upgrade of the water treatment plant, meaning the tax bills of every full-time island resident would be hiked to cover the cost. That would get Mary Jane voted out, so I heard she folded like a deck of cards under the pressure. And you did what?"

"I charged the privileged little shit," he said,

"although it didn't do any good. The DA has already thrown it out, calling me and chewing out my ass. But I made it clear to good old dad, who showed up here, breathing down my neck, that he's to keep his kid off the island, and if ever again we have a problem with him, a video of his racist diatribe will be all over the news."

She lifted her brows, leaned back, and crossed her feet on his desk, and he wasn't sure if she was amused. "You have a video?"

He reached for the baseball and the plaques and shoved them in the box. "No, but he doesn't know that. Anyway, I ordered a body camera for Carmen, and she'll wear it. The council will freak, mind you, when they get the bill, but I'm not having her credibility shredded because of some privileged kid who gets a free ride and thinks he can do anything he wants without consequence. Because her word won't count against his if shit hits the fan." He knew he was shoving everything in the box a little harder than necessary. "As far as Hal Green, I reminded him of all the tickets he had the chief write off for him over the years and let him know I have a copy of every one of them, including his emails to the chief telling him to take care of it."

Her expression was unreadable. "I thought you didn't keep any of the chief's insurance, the dirt he had on the council," she said. "You said you didn't want to operate that way."

Mark shrugged, thinking of the files in the bottom drawer, the proof of how Herb Walker had dipped into the funding for the island homeless, the tickets for Hal Green, and the photos of the head of the council herself, Mary Jane, with Philip Maddox, the reason the chief was no longer the chief. "If those running things actually played by the rules, I guess you and I wouldn't be having this conversation," he replied. "Didn't say I would use them, but I'd be stupid to throw them out."

She nodded. "Heard you eventually paid the license renewal fee for Grace Peters, too," she said. "Word gets around that you can't help being a good guy, Mark."

He only grunted. Aggressive prosecution against a woman who just couldn't afford her license didn't sit right with him. "She's got kids, no support, and her job barely pays her a living wage."

Billy Jo lifted her hands. "Hey, you don't need to justify it to me. I get it, Mark, and I'm behind you. I'm just saying that the council doesn't like being backed into a corner, and they especially don't like having a chief they can't control, so you'll need to watch your back. Now, those two, you should call them." She gestured to the two resumes she'd pulled out, Georgette Walker and Mike Schneider. One was from Salem, the other from Olympia. "And I'm starving, so how much more do you have to do?"

He took in the box, the girl, and the resumes on his desk. "Tons, but it'll keep." He reached for the pile of resumes and tossed them on top of the box. "For dinner, how about steak?"

She shrugged and stood up. "You're cooking?" She reached for her bag, and he took in the curves she was no longer hiding.

"Yeah. I'll throw steaks on the grill, and you can go through the rest of these resumes..." He lifted the box and started out of his office, following her.

"And the box?" She gestured back to him as he

flicked off the light with his elbow and whistled to Lucky, who was now up and striding to the door.

"I'll drop it off at the chief's," he said. "As you pointed out, these are his things."

She pulled open the door.

"Lock it, will you?" he said. "The keys are in my pocket."

She hesitated only a second before reaching into his pocket, a touch he hadn't expected, and she pulled the keys out. He strode to his Jeep and opened the back to stuff the box in, then grabbed the papers and pulled open the front door.

Billy Jo tossed him the keys, which he caught one-handed, before starting to her new Nissan Rogue. She would just follow him to his place, he knew, and he considered for a second this relationship they'd fallen into. Her place or his place didn't matter. It was always dinner, talking, and then he or she would leave. Maybe tonight he could figure out a way to change her mind and get her to stay.

About the Author

"Lorhainne Eckhart is one of my go to authors when I want a guaranteed good book. So many twists and turns, but also so much love and such a strong sense of family."

(Lora W., Reviewer)

New York Times & USA Today bestseller Lorhainne Eckhart writes Raw Relatable Real Romance is best known for her big family romances series, where "Morals and family are running themes. Danger, romance, and a drive to do what is right will see you glued to the page." As one fan calls her, she is the

"Queen of the family saga." (aherman) writing "the ups and downs of what goes on within a family but also with some suspense, angst and of course a bit of romance thrown in for good measure." Follow Lorhainne on Bookbub to receive alerts on New Releases and Sales and join her mailing list at LorhainneEckhart.com for her Monday Blog, books news, giveaways and FREE reads. With over 120 books, audiobooks, and multiple series published and available at all retailers now translated into six languages. She is a multiple recipient of the Readers' Favorite Award for Suspense and Romance, and lives in the Pacific Northwest on an island, is the mother of three, her oldest has autism and she is an advocate for never giving up on your dreams.

"Lorhainne Eckhart has this uncanny way of just hitting the spot every time with her books."

(Caroline L., Reviewer)

The O'Connells: *The O'Connells of Livingston, Montana are not your typical family. A riveting collection of stories surrounding the ups and downs of what goes on within a family but also with some suspense, angst and of course a bit of romance thrown in for good measure "I thought I loved the Friessens, but I absolutely adore the O'Connell's. Each and every book has totally different genres of stories but the one thing in common is how she is able to wrap it around the family which is the heart of each story." (C. Logue)*

The Friessens: *An emotional big family romance series, the Friessen family siblings find their relationships tested, lay their hearts on the line, and discover lasting love! "Lorhainne Eckhart is one of my go to authors when I want a guaranteed good book. So many twists and turns, but also so much love and such a strong sense of family." (Lora W., Reviewer)*

The Parker Sisters: *The Parker Sisters are a close-knit family, and like any other family they have their ups and downs. "Eckhart has crafted another intense family drama…The character development is outstanding, and the emotional investment is high…" (Aherman, Reviewer)*

The McCabe Brothers: *Join the five McCabe siblings on their journeys to the dark and dangerous side of love! An intense, exhilarating collection of romantic thrillers you won't want to miss. — "Eckhart has a new series that is definitely worth the read. The queen of the family saga started this series with a spin-off of her wildly successful Friessen series." From a Readers' Favorite award—winning author and "queen of the family saga" (Aherman)*

Lorhainne loves to hear from her readers! You can connect with me at:

www.LorhainneEckhart.com

lorhainneeckhart.le@gmail.com

Also by Lorhainne Eckhart

The Outsider Series
The Forgotten Child (Brad and Emily)
A Baby and a Wedding *(An Outsider Series Short)*
Fallen Hero (Andy, Jed, and Diana)
The Search *(An Outsider Series Short)*
The Awakening (Andy and Laura)
Secrets (Jed and Diana)
Runaway (Andy and Laura)
Overdue *(An Outsider Series Short)*
The Unexpected Storm (Neil and Candy)
The Wedding (Neil and Candy)

The Friessens: A New Beginning
The Deadline (Andy and Laura)
The Price to Love (Neil and Candy)
A Different Kind of Love (Brad and Emily)
A Vow of Love, A Friessen Family Christmas

The Friessens
The Reunion
The Bloodline (Andy & Laura)
The Promise (Diana & Jed)
The Business Plan (Neil & Candy)
The Decision (Brad & Emily)
First Love (Katy)
Family First
Leave the Light On
In the Moment

In the Family
In the Silence
In the Charm
Unexpected Consequences
It Was Always You
The First Time I Saw You
Welcome to My Arms
Welcome to Boston
I'll Always Love You
Ground Rules
A Reason to Breathe
You Are My Everything
Anything For You
The Homecoming
Stay Away From My Daughter
The Bad Boy
A Place of Our Own
The Visitor
All About Devon
Long Past Dawn
How to Heal a Heart
Keep Me In Your Heart

The O'Connells
The Neighbor
The Third Call
The Secret Husband
The Quiet Day
The Commitment
The Missing Father
The Hometown Hero
Justice
The Family Secret

The Fallen O'Connell
The Return of the O'Connells
And The She Was Gone
The Stalker
The O'Connell Family Christmas
The Girl Next Door
Broken Promises
The Gatekeeper

The McCabe Brothers
Don't Stop Me (Vic)
Don't Catch Me (Chase)
Don't Run From Me (Aaron)
Don't Hide From Me (Luc)
Don't Leave Me (Claudia)
Out of Time

A Billy Jo McCabe Mystery
Nothing As it Seems
Hiding in Plain Sight
The Cold Case
The Trap
Above the Law
The Stranger at the Door
The Children
The Last Stand

The Street Fighter
Finding Home

The Wilde Brothers
The One (Joe and Margaret)
The Honeymoon, A Wilde Brothers Short

Friendly Fire (Logan and Julia)
Not Quite Married, A Wilde Brothers Short
A Matter of Trust (Ben and Carrie)
The Reckoning, A Wilde Brothers Christmas
Traded (Jake)
Unforgiven (Samuel)
The Holiday Bride

Married in Montana
His Promise
Love's Promise
A Promise of Forever

The Parker Sisters
Thrill of the Chase
The Dating Game
Play Hard to Get
What We Can't Have
Go Your Own Way
A June Wedding

Kate & Walker
One Night
Edge of Night
Last Night

Walk the Right Road Series
The Choice
Lost and Found
Merkaba
Bounty
Blown Away: The Final Chapter

The Saved Series
Saved
Vanished
Captured

Single Titles
He Came Back
Loving Christine

For my German Readers
Die Außenseiter-Reihe
Der Vergessene Junge
Der Gefallene Held

For my French Readers
L'ENFANT OUBLIÉ

www.ingramcontent.com/pod-product-compliance
Lightning Source LLC
Chambersburg PA
CBHW030944210726
48290CB00007B/2325